D A T E D U E		

Also by Nancy Garden

Annie on My Mind

Prisoner of Vampires

Peace, O River

What Happened in Marston

Berlin: City Split in Two

The Loners

Vampires

Werewolves

Witches

Devils and Demons

The Kids' Code and Cipher Book

THE FOURS CROSSING BOOKS

Fours Crossing

Watersmeet

The Door Between

THE MONSTER HUNTERS SERIES

Mystery of the Night Raiders

Mystery of the Midnight Menace

Mystery of the Secret Marks

Lark in the Morning

Lark in the Morning

NANCY GARDEN

Farrar Straus Giroux

New York

Excerpts from "East Coker" and "Burnt Norton" in *Four Quartets*, copyright 1943 by T. S. Eliot and renewed 1971 by Esme Valerie Eliot, reprinted by permission of Harcourt Brace Jovanovich, Inc.

For all of us—again

Lark in the Morning

One

LATE-AFTERNOON SUN slanted through fragile leaves, painting dappled birch trunks with gold. Gillian Harrison—Gillian with a hard *g*—climbed eagerly over the jumble of suitcases and cartons in the back seat of her parents' Toyota and stood next to its open door, savoring the quiet. As always, she felt mildly surprised and very grateful that the woods was still there, along with the lake and the small board-and-batten cabin that felt more like home to her than the New York City apartment she and her parents had left that morning.

Her mother's voice, fear under its urgency, cut into the stillness. "Alex! Wait! Come look at this!"

Professor Harrison put down the two suitcases he had taken out of the car's trunk and strode briskly down the rough flagstone path to the cabin. Gillian followed. Her mother had dropped the wooden case containing her paints, and was pointing shakily at scratch marks in the faded red back door, near the lock.

"It looks as if someone tried to force it," said the professor.

"I think someone did force it," Mrs. Harrison whispered, turning the knob. "It's not locked anymore."

"Mom, wait," Gillian urged, but her mother had already released the knob without opening the door. "Shouldn't we get the police or something?"

"Yes, of course." But Mrs. Harrison still stood there, as if unable to move.

"Come on, Barb." Calmly, the professor put a hand on his wife's shoulder. "Let's go. If nothing else, it'll give whoever it is a chance to get out if they're still there."

All three Harrisons hurried to the Toyota. Professor Harrison stuffed the two suitcases back into the trunk, and Gillian squeezed into the rear seat, scraping her foot against her father's typewriter, on the floor amid a pile of sneakers. Mrs. Harrison, clutching her paint case and her straw summer pocketbook, slid into the front, gingerly, as if even sliding might make too much noise.

The Harrisons had been spending their summers in Pookatasset, Rhode Island, for the past five years, ever since Professor Harrison had inherited some money and bought the cabin and the ten acres surrounding it; that had been the year Gillian was twelve and her sister Margie was sixteen. Margie had come only briefly most summers, preferring to work at summer-stock theaters instead, but Gillian couldn't imagine being anywhere else between late June and early September.

"I suppose we're lucky," Mrs. Harrison said nervously, turning to Gillian while the professor, his lean face looking leaner than usual now that his jaw was set with worry, steered skillfully down the winding dirt driveway. Gillian and Margie used to kid their parents for being like Jack Sprat and his wife, but lately Gillian had realized she and Margie were like that, too. Gillian, darker and thinner than her sister, favored their father more and more each year, while Margie was fair like their mother and, like her, constantly had to be careful of her weight.

"Ever since we've had this place," Mrs. Harrison went on, "I've wondered why no one's broken in. I just hope they didn't do any damage, or take anything."

"Oh, but that's the point, isn't it?" said the professor with light sarcasm. "To take things or tear them apart. Fun, I believe they call it."

"Sometimes people break in just to—you know. Use the house," said his wife.

Gillian visualized a couple of teenagers huddled in her parents' queen-sized bed, terrified as the car drove up, and scrambling to dress and run out now that it had left. But where would they run to? Not down the dirt drive, probably; what if the Harrisons anticipated that, and waited for them? Deeper into the woods, perhaps; maybe as far as the old abandoned hut Gillian and, once in a while, Margie, had used for sleepovers when they'd been younger. Or they could have gone down to the lake; maybe the couple had a boat hidden . . .

The Pookatasset police station was only a couple of miles from the cabin, past the grange, a house or two, and the big farm where Brad Finnegan, Gillian's best Pookatasset friend since that first summer, lived. Professor Harrison turned out onto the main road, muttering as he did every summer about needing to prune the bushes on the corner to improve visibility. Maybe I'll do it for him, Gillian mused; her father was more comfortable with his books and his typewriter than with tools. It was Gillian who did most of the outdoor work around the cabin, even cutting firewood, having convinced her parents a couple of years ago that she could handle the bow saw.

What if whoever had broken in had actually stolen something? What if they'd taken *Sprite*, the rowboat, from under the house? Or found the secret closet under the stairs where her parents stored valuables for the winter: the TV, the ceramic lamps her mother had made during her pottery period, the heater they used on chilly nights, and the few tools too expensive to keep in the shed—the chain saw Gillian still wasn't allowed to use; the electric drill? And the oars—not valuable but precious.

Don't let them have taken *Sprite*, Gillian prayed, knowing the rowboat was the one thing she'd miss badly. Theoretically, *Sprite* belonged to the whole family, but it had been Gillian who'd named her, and Gillian who'd always used her most, rowing across the lake to the village for mail and groceries before she was able to drive, and spending hours exploring the long, jagged shoreline or just drifting on the lake whenever she wanted to be alone.

She'd wanted to be alone more and more lately, and had been especially looking forward to long rows in *Sprite* this summer, without even Brad for company, and maybe even without being too lonely for Suzanne Morris, the only person who could make her want to stay in New York. Suzanne would be visiting in a few days, anyway, on the July Fourth weekend, as she always did.

"Here we are," announced Professor Harrison unnecessarily as he turned into a newly blacktopped parking lot bordered with young petunias in railroad-tie beds. He drove past the first building—the volunteer fire department's garage—and parked at one side of the low brick structure that contained the town offices as well as the police station. It was behind an overgrown array of yews and arborvitae, and was almost invisible from the road, but as Brad often said, there was so little crime in Pookatasset that the town barely needed police, let alone an obvious place in which to house them.

"Everyone coming?" asked the professor.

Mrs. Harrison nodded, and followed; Gillian followed her.

Inside the police section of the building was a small dark hallway with a glassless interior window cut into one wall and a counter protruding from it, as if the piece of wall removed for the window had simply been folded down to make a shelf.

Behind the opening was a stout woman in a police uniform.

"So," said the professor, after introducing himself and explaining about the forced door, "we thought it might be smarter to come here first, in case whoever broke in was still there and feeling, shall we say, edgy."

"Quite right," said the woman. "I'll get a couple of

officers to go down with you. We've had a few break-ins lately, as a matter of fact—unusual for us, mind you; you'd think we were turning into a city. They've mostly been summer places like yours, at least so far. But you never can tell where something like this'll lead, once it starts. Excuse me." She turned away and Gillian could hear her speaking to someone, though she couldn't make out the words. Then the woman came back, saying, "Officers Harper and Dolan will be right with you." She put her arms on the counter and leaned forward confidentially. "There've been some thefts, just minor things, from the other places—probably kids, not real thieves. Still, nice start to the summer, isn't it?" she added, with an ironic smile at Mrs. Harrison. "But, like I said, none of the break-ins have been very serious. Maybe you'll be lucky, too."

"I hope so," said Mrs. Harrison. Then she glanced from a clock on the wall to her watch. "What time," she asked her husband, "did Margie say she and Peter were coming?"

"I don't think she did say," he answered. "Sometime before dinner. Barbara, it's only four."

"I'm just worried she'll go there and barge in."

"She's got too much brain for that. Besides, Peter's both levelheaded and strong. She'll be all right."

Strong, Gillian thought, doesn't quite say it. Margie's steady boyfriend was, as Margie often put it, a "hunk"; he worked out with weights and bench-pressed 250 pounds. He was so friendly most people got along with him easily, herself included; Gillian was, in fact, very fond of him. And, as her father had pointed out, he was levelheaded.

Two policemen came out of a back room, one with

a heavy, coarse face so red it looked sunburned, and the other lantern-jawed, with kind eyes, at least.

"Officer Harper," said the woman, nodding toward the red-faced one; his meaty hands were red, too, Gillian noticed, so maybe it was indeed sunburn. "And Officer Dolan, our youth officer."

Youth Officer Dolan bowed his head gravely; Officer Harper held out his hand to Gillian's father and said, "We'll follow you, sir, shall we?"

"Not much of a welcome for you, is it?" Officer Dolan said conversationally to Mrs. Harrison as they all trooped out to the parking lot; that theme, Gillian thought as she got back into the Toyota, is beginning to get a bit overworked.

The police officers actually drew their revolvers as they opened the cabin's back door, having instructed the Harrisons to wait in the Toyota. Luckily, Margie and Peter had not yet arrived.

"I suppose," said Mrs. Harrison tensely as the officers went inside, weapons bristling, "that the guns are a necessary precaution, and I guess we should be grateful, but it does seem melodramatic. I mean, here it is, a nice sunny afternoon in quiet little Pookatasset. It's hard to believe any of this is happening. You don't suppose they'll actually use the guns, Alex, do you?"

"I doubt it," the professor answered. "As I think I mentioned, anyone who was here when we arrived would have been a fool to stay. Anyway, it won't take the police long to search, I'm sure. It'll be okay, Barb; don't worry so much."

A few minutes later, Officer Harper came out and

somehow forced his rotund body under the house. The three-foot-high crawl space there was where *Sprite* was stored, along with ladders, old window frames, and other large odds and ends.

"You have just the one boat?" he called, easing himself out and standing up with a grunt. One of his sleeves had come unbuttoned and had pushed up; sunburn, Gillian decided definitely. Funny what one notices, she thought as she called, "Yes, just one." Obviously, *Sprite* was still there.

"Well, she looks okay. Guess you folks can come in now," he added after his partner had appeared at the door and had spoken to him briefly. "No sign of anyone," he said as the Harrisons approached. "And no sign of any damage, either."

"Thank goodness." Relief was almost palpable in Mrs. Harrison's voice.

"A couple of cupboards are open, though," Youth Officer Dolan said, his squared-off face looking grave. "You'd better check, ma'am, to see if anything's missing."

They all went inside; the back door led right into the kitchen. "Something thin was passed between the door and its jamb, against the lock," Officer Harper explained. "It's an old lock, too, loose-fitting—not too hard to force, I imagine. You might think about replacing it."

"Yes." The professor sighed. "It's one of those things I've been meaning to do, I'm afraid."

"Luckily, we don't leave much here over the winter," Mrs. Harrison told the police when they were all inside and she had begun looking into cupboards; the professor moved quietly into the living room, heading,

Gillian knew, for his study. Officer Harper followed him. "So there's not much to take."

"Those metal boxes of pasta," said Gillian, searching in the far cabinet. "Remember? The red-and-blue ones Aunt Hattie gave us? They were full, I think, one with spaghetti and one with macaroni. They're not here."

"You're right," said her mother. "And"—she looked into another cupboard—"there was some cocoa mix, I think, and a little instant coffee."

Youth Officer Dolan, leaning up against the counter by the wall phone, made a note.

"And the dog biscuits," said Gillian. "Remember? From when Peter brought his dog at the end of last summer, and Margie wanted to leave the biscuits here as a sign he'd come back—Peter, I mean, not necessarily the dog."

"Everything's okay in the study, Barb," the professor called from his small cavelike room off the combination living room and dining room that opened onto a wide screened-in porch overlooking the lake. "And the under-the-stairs closet is intact. Oars are still there, Gillie."

"Thanks, Dad," Gillian called back. "Okay if I check upstairs?" she asked Officer Dolan, and when he agreed, she hurried up to the balcony that ran around the upper part of the main room, whose cathedral ceiling rose all the way to the roof. There were four compact bedrooms off the balcony, one on each side: her parents', hers, Margie's, and a guest room.

She saved her room for last, wanting to greet it specially, but the others all seemed fine.

"Looks like there are a couple of towels missing,"

11

she heard her mother say from the bathroom, which was downstairs. "Yes, I'm sure of it. Those big rough blue ones, Margie's favorites. What a pity!"

On an impulse, Gillian went to the blanket chest on the stair landing.

Usually it was bursting and popped right open when touched, as if happy to be freed from the pressure beneath. But Gillian could see that the lid fit more snugly than usual, and as soon as she lifted it, she saw there was a big space at the top. "Mom, how many blankets do we have?" she called, counting.

"Oh, heavens, I don't know. A dozen, maybe."

"Well, I think there's one or two missing."

Mrs. Harrison came up the stairs and looked down into the chest, then knelt and riffled through the remaining blankets. "Yes, you're right, Gillie. That thick brown one's gone, and the lighter blue one." Gillian saw her mother's eyes fill with tears.

"Two blankets, right?" said Officer Dolan briskly; he had followed Mrs. Harrison upstairs with the clipboard on which he'd been noting missing items. "One blue, one brown, right?"

Mrs. Harrison nodded and turned away; Gillian closed the chest's lid.

"Maybe you'd better check closets," Officer Harper said from the foot of the stairs.

"Yes, I guess you're right." Mrs. Harrison stood up, appearing to rally. "Thank goodness we don't have many clothes here," she said, disappearing into her room. "Just a few bathing suits and ratty old sweaters."

Gillian heard her mother open a closet door; she said, "Excuse me" to Officer Dolan and squeezed past him, heading for her own room.

Coming into her cabin room each summer was like saying hello to an old friend. It was as much a haven for her as were the woods and lake—more, in a way, since it had always been hers alone. In New York, she'd shared a room with Margie till Margie had gone to college; for the last four years, many of Margie's belongings had been stored there, and Margie still slept there on vacations. But Gillian had never had to share her cabin room unless she wanted to.

Its windows, with a full bookcase between them, looked out over the lake, from which bullfrogs regularly sang her to sleep. As she lay in bed on moonlit nights and in the early mornings, she could look up at the branches of a huge hemlock that grew by the porch, making endlessly intricate shadows on the walls and sometimes even on the wide red floorboards. The paint on the floor was shiny enough to reflect moonbeams and sunbeams as well as light from the small electric lamp on her desk and the other one over her bed.

But the thing that made her room most special was on the wall behind the desk, where there hung an old calendar picture of a barn and some cows, in a birchbark frame Gillian had made when she was thirteen. Behind it, and the reason for both picture and frame, was a hole she had cut secretly into the plasterboard wall. She'd anchored a large tin box to the studs she'd exposed, to make a storage place safe from her then-nosy sister. For the last couple of years, she'd kept her summer diary in it—and she'd left last summer's there, thinking it would be safer in the unoccupied cabin than in New York, where she had no truly private place. Even though Margie was gone most of the year, Gillian was never sure that either she or their

13

mother wouldn't be tempted to at least glance at the diary if it was out in the open. And last summer's diary was one she didn't want anyone to see.

Now, anxious to reread what she'd written a year ago, Gillian closed the door, lifted the cow picture off the wall—and stared in stunned disbelief into the empty box.

Two

GILLIAN TUGGED *Sprite*'s bow around to face the narrow beach she, Margie, and their father had scooped out long ago between two pines and a tupelo tree on the shore. Then, with some effort, she flipped the boat over and inspected her bottom. Not bad, considering *Sprite* had been under the house all winter, a home for mice and squirrels, no doubt, and prey to cycles of damping and drying. The bottom could use a coat of paint, and there was a suspicious-looking thin crack beginning right next to the ridge that passed for a keel, but Gillian was too impatient to see to it now, and she knew the crack would swell closed anyway, as soon as *Sprite* was wet enough.

Gillian flipped the boat right-side-up again, tossed in the oars, the anchor, and a coffee-can bailer, took off her shoes, and slid *Sprite* into the lake. Then she climbed aboard and poled to water deep enough to row in.

"Come back," her mother had said, "as soon as you hear me call. Better yet, I'll honk the car horn when Margie and Peter get here."

Gillian was sure there'd be plenty of time; Margie was never very prompt when she was with Peter.

It was a perfect afternoon. The lake was smooth and lazy, its surface broken only by an occasional water bug or dragonfly. A hawk circled silently overhead, then disappeared in the marshy spot far to the left of the Harrisons' cabin. Points, inlets, bays, curves; Gillian smiled, reviewing in her mind those portions of the ragged shoreline she couldn't see. Most of the lakeside houses, like the Harrisons', were hidden by trees and by blueberry and sweet-pepper bushes, except for two pretentious stucco mansions on the other side, with wide treeless lawns, out of place and ridiculous in the otherwise unspoiled setting. Almost everyone who lived on the lake respected its natural beauty and disrupted it as little as possible. The only people who owned motorboats were the people in the mansions. Everyone else rowed, sailed, or canoed.

Gillian rowed to the center of the lake and sat scanning what was visible from there of the familiar shore, letting the lake's peacefulness wash over her worry about the missing diary. The old maple on the point near the marsh still looked healthy, and the sweet-pepper thickets were heavy with buds. The usual lily pads choked the entrance to the marsh, and the flat rocks opposite it, baking in the sun, gave off faint wiggles of warm air, rising vertically like visible sound waves. Only someone who knew this shore as well as Gillian could make out the grassy or pine-needled paths that led from the lake to the widely spaced cabins around it—which makes it unlikely, she thought, for whoever broke in to have come by water, unless they knew their way around.

Why would anyone want someone else's diary?

And how had they discovered it? Bumped into the picture, dislodging it, and then, after stealing the diary, taken the time to replace the picture properly?

Would a thief read someone else's diary?

But why else take it? Embarrassment flooded her when she thought about some of what she'd written. She'd referred to the difficult part obliquely most of the time as "The Problem," but it was pretty clear what it was. And even though it was no longer a problem in the same way, it was still no one's business but hers and Suzanne's.

Of course, she'd written less private things in the diary, too, about choosing colleges, and about all the arguments she'd had with her parents over wanting to go to forestry school instead of to regular college. She'd won that one, finally, and was slated to go to Oregon State's—on four hundred acres, between two mountain ranges, the catalogue said—in September. Gillian had pictured herself, ever since the acceptance came, with backpack and sleeping bag, hiking through those mountains, learning to rock-climb, maybe, swinging herself over crags with only a rope and perhaps one other person between her and disaster . . .

"Hi, there, Gillie!"

Brad Finnegan's yellow punt was scudding toward her, battered but serviceable, and Brad, his rugged tan face split with the little-kid grin that rarely failed to cheer her, was rowing rapidly with the long easy strokes she'd always admired and often tried to imitate.

"So you're here." He angled broadside to her and backed water to keep his boat in position.

"Looks it," said Gillian, returning his grin, glad to see him. He hadn't changed much—filled out some, perhaps, if that was possible; he'd always been strong and sturdy, though stockier than Peter, and smaller, less obviously muscular.

"What's this about a break-in?"

"Wow, news travels fast!" She told him about it, but not about the diary. She hadn't told her parents that, either, or the police.

"There've been others," he said, as the police had done. "A couple of summer cabins. That youth officer guy, Dolan, thinks it's probably kids. Nothing much has been taken; food, mostly. Lots of dog food from one place."

"That's funny," said Gillian thoughtfully. "They took biscuits left over from Peter's dog."

"They must have a dog then, or be mighty hungry. Brilliant deduction, right? They took a couple of plates from one cabin," Brad went on. "And forks and knives and spoons. Cups, too. Just a couple, like they were setting up very limited housekeeping. Reform school ought to be their next stop, if you ask me." Brad's grin broadened. "My arms are tired. How about we tie *Sprite* to my boat and you climb aboard?"

She agreed, and he held her hand a moment longer than necessary when she crawled over to his boat. "I've missed you," he said. "More than usual. Welcome back."

"I've missed you, too," she admitted. But she moved away quickly, busying herself with *Sprite*'s bow line, conscious of how he'd held her hand.

He watched her. Then he said, "I guess I'd better ask the obvious question. Get it over with fast."

"What's that?" But she knew. Well, as he said, better get it over with.

"Suzanne. I kept wondering all winter. You never said in your letters."

"I still love her, if that's what you mean. I didn't say because I wasn't sure how to tell you, how you'd react." She coiled the last of the bow line. Its tip needed rewhipping; she'd have to see to that soon.

"You didn't know how I'd react?" He smiled ruefully. "You with that soft black hair and pixie face; those quiet eyes; that exasperating inscrutability? One never knows what you're up to, Gill. You loved Suzanne last summer. Have you told her, I meant?"

She looked up from the rope. "Yes, I've told her. I didn't till December, but I told her then."

"Well? What happened? Or"—he moved away slightly—"or maybe it's none of my business."

"No, no," she said quickly. "Of course it is. It's just that—that I haven't talked about it to anyone. And . . ."

"And I have a sort of a vested interest. Or did. I know. That makes it harder. But I guess I expected you'd still feel the same. I'd rather be your friend than lose you, Gillian."

"Sure?"

"Sure. You're special to me. I've never known a girl I could talk to the way I can to you. I kind of figured, with what you didn't say in your letters, that friends was as far as it would go with us. Maybe I'll hope some, but . . ."

"Don't, Brad. Don't hope. Please. I care about you

19

a lot. I don't want to lose you either, as a friend. But I'm not going to change. Last summer I wasn't all that sure. But Suzanne and I—we're lovers now." She smiled at him shyly. "It's the best thing that's ever happened to me."

"I guess I'm glad for you," he said, but stiffly. Then he paused, hesitating. "Are you still going to Oregon?"

"I have to. I'll miss her, she'll miss me, but we—what we feel for each other—is so strong it's overpowering—scary, sometimes. We—need space, maybe."

He looked at her oddly. "Seems to me if you love each other that much, you ought to be together."

"How can we? She's going to art school; I'm going to forestry school; our parents . . ."

"Do they know? Your folks? Margie?"

"No."

"They should, Gillie, if it's so important to you."

"I know, but I don't want to hurt them."

"Maybe it wouldn't."

"That's for me to decide. Brad—I'll tell them, but in my own time. I'm hoping they'll figure it out, someday."

"Okay. I didn't mean to butt in. Hey, look! There's that old hawk." He pointed.

Gillian looked up gratefully. "Yes," she said. "I saw him a few minutes ago. I guess he's going to live forever, if he's the same one that's always here." She paused, then said, "How about you? Judy, wasn't it?"

"*Wasn't* is right. It's Michelle now."

"Serious? Do I know her?"

"I don't think so, to both. How could it be serious when I wasn't sure about you yet?"

"I'm sorry, Brad."

"What would you say," he asked, leaning forward, "if I got a job out in Oregon this fall? I've been thinking about it for a while. I'm not sure I want to start college yet, anyway."

"I'd question your motives," she answered gently. "And, last I heard, you were eager to go to college. URI. Agriculture. To learn what you already know how to do." She smiled. It was an old joke of theirs.

"That's just the point," he said. "I don't have to go to school to learn how to run Dad's farm. I've watched him all my life, and I can raise anything he can raise in my sleep with one hand tied, et cetera. No, I'd go to Oregon with you—no strings, Gillian, I mean it—and do something else."

"Like what?"

"Like I don't know. Lumber, maybe. Or fish. It doesn't matter. I could pick up farming again whenever I came back. Like you, maybe I need space."

"But it wouldn't be space for me if we were there together. Maybe not for you, either, aside from farming. You know it wouldn't."

"Even if we didn't see each other much? We wouldn't, if I was fishing or lumbering."

"Brad, no. I really need to be far away, from everyone. I'd much rather you didn't come."

"Even far away from Suzanne? Are you sure of that?"

"Yes. As I said, I'll miss her, but I've known her forever, longer than I've known you. We need to be two people, if we can; we need to grow up away from each other a little. You and me, too. I'll write, I promise. I can't keep you from going to Oregon, or anywhere. But if you do go, I won't see you, so . . ."

"So if that's why I'm going, I shouldn't bother." He

sighed. "You're probably right. Are you really sure, though?"

She looked away over the lake; the hawk had stopped circling and was perched at the edge of the marsh. "Yes," she said emphatically. "I'm really sure."

Three

IT MIGHT BE EASIER now, with Brad, Gillian thought as she rowed back. Last summer had been tense once he'd begun wanting to be more than friends, and stormy at first when she'd finally told him about Suzanne and The Problem. And even though in time he'd seemed to accept her confusion, and even though he'd tried to understand, she'd felt him hovering over her emotionally, slowing himself down while he waited for a decision from her.

She hated hurting him, hurting anyone.

Gillian shipped her oars. A fish jumped, and she envied it its freedom enough to drop the anchor overboard, shuck off her shoes, and dive in; she was wearing shorts and a T-shirt—nothing much to drag her down.

The water was wonderfully cold and sparkling. Below the surface, the lake was clear, and for a while she watched two fish circling each other in panic at

23

her interruption. Too soon, she ached for air and had to come up, reluctantly breaking the thin line between lake and sky.

She shook the water out of her ears and dove back under, scrabbling along the bottom this time, finding stones, weeds, an old glass bottle filled with sand.

I didn't want, she thought, to have to battle anything or anyone this summer. But I know I don't want Brad trailing me out to Oregon. If anyone, I'd want Suze, but the art teachers she wants to study with are in New York. And we do need space.

She came up, swam slowly back to *Sprite*, and, treading water, held herself steady with a hand on one gunwale till she'd caught her breath, thinking: We can't stop being ourselves, Suze and I, just because we love each other and want to be together. It'd end then, surely. And I need to know who I am, just me, by myself.

The car horn sounded as she beached *Sprite* and, glad of the distraction Margie and Peter would provide, she ran up the path, still dripping water.

They were standing on the porch, looking out over the lake.

Margie whooped and ran to her, folding her in a bear hug, then held her at arms' length, laughing. "You're a sight, Gill," she said. "Pretty sexy in that wet shirt. Peter, look the other way."

Peter, making an elaborate show of closing his eyes, held out his enormous hand. "Hi, Gillian," he said. "Fall overboard, did you? Close encounter of the sea kind?"

Gillian punched his arm playfully instead of shak-

24

ing his hand. "Right," she said. "Lake, not sea. But you should see the people in the other boat."

"Good lord, Gillian!" exclaimed Mrs. Harrison, coming onto the porch. "Do run up and change!"

"Yes'm." Gillian touched her forehead as if tipping a cap, and cheerfully went upstairs.

She was standing naked in her room drying herself when Margie knocked and said, "Decent?"

"No." Gillian reached for her clothes as Margie came in.

"Did you really fall overboard?" asked Margie, sitting down on Gillian's bed and curling her short legs under her. Her sister's quiet, fair face was still winter-pale, Gillian noticed, even though she knew her own had already darkened some in the hot city sun.

"No, of course not. Pirate Gill doesn't fall overboard."

Margie laughed. The reference was to a long-dead game, played at Gillian's insistence their first summer at the cabin, in which Gillian was a pirate captain and Margie was everyone else, including victims; the lake was the Spanish Main.

"I didn't think so," said Margie.

"I just went for a swim." Gillian pulled on a dry T-shirt.

Margie raised her eyebrows. "Accoutered as you were?"

"Right." Margie was known for quoting obscure lines from Shakespeare. She'd been a theater major in college and wanted to be an actress. In fact, she'd met Peter at a summer-stock playhouse where he was stage manager and where Margie, still in high school,

25

was an apprentice. They'd worked at separate theaters since then, but had been hired by the same one this season, and so would be living and working about a half hour's drive from Pookatasset, on the Rhode Island shore. " 'Accoutered as I was,' " Gillian quoted, " 'I plungéd in.' Brad and I just had a talk, and I needed cheering up. Or maybe cooling down."

Margie raised her eyebrows again.

Gillian sat down next to her. "Brad says he wants to get a job in Oregon next fall, instead of going to URI."

"To be near you, right?"

"Right."

"And you said?"

"I said no. I don't want him to come."

"He's a nice guy, Gill."

"I know."

"But?"

"But I don't feel that way about him."

"Then tell him."

"I did."

"Oh, Gillie!" Margie put her arm around Gillian. "And you split up?"

"No," said Gillian, momentarily astonished. "No, of course not."

Now Margie looked astonished. "You mean you're going to go on seeing each other?"

"Well, sure. We're friends; we've always been friends. Why shouldn't we?"

"Is that fair to him? I mean, he's going to go on hoping, Gillian; that's inevitable."

"But I *told* him, and . . ." She broke off. "I know. You're probably right. But he wants to see me. And I want to see him."

"Just don't be a tease, Gillie, okay? That's the worst thing to be."

Gillian looked at her quizzically.

"I'm sorry, but that's what it sounds like to me. Don't hurt a nice guy. They don't come much nicer, except for Peter, of course." She stood up. "What a funny bug you are, Gillian. I'm going down to help Mom with dinner. Come soon?"

"Sure," Gillian said, troubled. "Margie? It seems to me that if we do go on seeing each other, he'll have more of a chance to see how I really feel. Or how I don't feel. No?"

Margie shook her head, more in exasperation, Gillian felt, than denial. "Funny bug," she said again, and left.

After dinner, the police called to make sure the Harrisons hadn't found anything else missing, stressing that the kind of thing taken might be a clue as to who had broken in. Gillian guiltily, and with considerable embarrassment, mentioned her diary, and when she got off the phone, her mother said "Diary? I didn't know you kept one." Peter must have sensed her discomfort, for he remarked tactfully, "I didn't hear anything about a diary. You, Margie?" Margie shook her head, though she looked curious, and no more was said.

But Gillian, as she did the dishes, having volunteered in order to give Margie and Peter the time alone with her parents that they seemed to want, couldn't forget about it, and about the fact that a stranger might be reading about her most private self. At least, she reasoned, whoever took the diary won't know who Suzanne is, or me either.

Suzanne Morris had been Gillian's friend starting in sixth grade. They'd met on West 98th Street in Manhattan, in the elevator of the apartment building in which both their families lived. The Morrises had moved downtown when Suzanne and Gillian were fourteen, but Suze insisted on going to the same high school as Gillian, and they'd grown steadily closer. Then one night in the spring of junior year, she and Gillian, in a silly, giddy mood, had started fooling around, mock wrestling and kidding each other about boys.

And Gillian had been just relaxed enough or just off-guard enough to let a wrestling hold turn into a hug, and to kiss her best friend, surprising herself as much with the rightness of it as with the fact that she'd done it.

At first, Suzanne had responded. But then she'd pulled away.

For months, though, Gillian could still feel Suzanne's mouth on hers.

They hadn't spoken of it.

But from then on Gillian had felt more than a little awkward around Suzanne. Suzanne, bouncy, cheerful, happy-go-lucky Suzanne, had gone right on in her usual way, dating and partying, maybe even more than before. Gillian had never done that, despite her mother's and sister's urging, so she knew it wouldn't seem odd if she didn't start—and Suzanne didn't push her. Suzanne had always accepted her the way she was, but Gillian didn't dare confide in her anymore, and after Suzanne's annual summer visit, which was strained on both their parts, she poured out her feelings in her diary and eventually talked to Brad.

That fall, she read everything she could find about

homosexuality, and finally, just before Christmas, she told Suzanne how she felt. Suzanne had burst into tears, terrifying Gillian, but it turned out they were tears of relief and joy. Her dating, she said, had been a cover; she'd felt the same way but had been afraid, because of Gillian's silence, that Gillian didn't, and had thought that Gillian would be disgusted if she knew.

Suzanne continued her cover for a while, but eventually stopped dating, saying to everyone except Gillian that she needed more time, more quiet, for painting. Gillian's own mother, since she painted herself, was one of Suzanne's staunchest supporters, and before long, everyone seemed to accept the new, no-longer-boy-crazy Suzanne.

How detailed, Gillian wondered, drying the last plate and putting it away, was what I wrote about The Problem in the diary back when it was a problem?

She went outside, launched *Sprite*, and rowed quietly out onto the moonlit water, then lay back and looked up at the stars, letting the boat drift, remembering when The Problem eased . . .

Remembering the night last winter when Suzanne's parents were away and she'd slept at Suzanne's apartment, in her bed for the first time . . .

Remembering the few times since then, no more than two or three, when they'd been able to touch, to explore the wonder of each other's bodies . . .

Remembering their talks, deeper now that they were lovers, their plans: Suzanne would go to art school for the requisite two years, then join Gillian in Oregon; they would live off campus while Gillian finished college; they would somehow explain to their parents. "I don't want us to be cut off from other people," Gillian had said, "just because we're gay and in love." And Suzanne had agreed.

It was getting harder, though, to stick to that . . .

Gillian sat up, blinking, dazed with her memories, reluctant to leave them. But surely that was a light in the woods, bobbing near the shore where it bent into a tiny bay about a quarter of a mile to the left of the beach, not far from the old hut where she and Margie had played years earlier. It was bobbing as if someone were walking there with a flashlight.

Now the light was still, focused down, as if the someone were looking for something. Then it went out, and there was a splash, followed by a suppressed laugh and another splash.

Someone skinny-dipping? But who? No one lived there.

Unless someone was using the hut?

They'd be trespassing, of course; the hut was on the edge of the Harrisons' land. But who would want to use it? Last summer when she had walked over the soggy path to it and forced the door open, the smell of mouse droppings and decay had almost choked her. The place was full of dust and cobwebs and lord knows what; she'd pulled the door closed again in a hurry and left.

Suppose it was the robbers?

Don't be silly, Gillian, she scolded herself. It's probably just children out late, playing. Or local teenagers. No need to make a fuss about it.

Besides, I can always check it out in the morning.

The light went on again, and bobbed away from the water, back into the woods.

30

Four

THE NEXT MORNING, Gillian found that the path to the hut was just as soggy as she remembered it; many of the boards she and her father had laid between stones in the muddier spots a couple of years ago were spongy, almost rotted away. Gillian had to hop from stone to stone in some places, or detour up to the higher side, to avoid sinking ankle-deep in mud and water.

But it was lovely, even so, in the early morning.

Laurel bushes edged the path where it was nearest the house, and a few delicately complicated white-and-pink blossoms still clung to the ends of branches. Yellow clintonias bobbed at the ends of their spikes, and in the drier sections, small yellow-and-white flowers, like ragged miniature daisies, peeked above the grass. Farther along, stubby jacks-in-the-pulpit sat in puddled pools, addressing congregations of spent marsh marigolds. Bees hovered over the sweet-pepper bushes, as if waiting impatiently for the buds to open.

A cicada's hum joined the bees'; it was going to be a hot day. Humid, too; already Gillian felt moisture rising from the swamp and collecting around it.

She detoured up to the high side of the path again, vowing to replace the boards and build bridges, make that a summer project along with pruning the bushes near the road. Then even the high side got muddy and she was forced to pause before a particularly wet section. The board spanning the more than path-wide rivulet that had stopped her looked free of rot, but she saw just in time that it was floating as well as slimy. If she stepped on it, it would go under, probably. Maybe she could jump.

She did, and nearly made the distance, but her feet landed too far apart. One foot slid on the slippery edge of the rivulet and was instantly mud-covered.

"Blast it!" she exclaimed aloud; she'd gotten a long scratch, too, on the back of one forearm where she'd crashed into a thorny bush.

At least, she thought, scraping mud off her foot with a stick, I can always wash my sneaker. And the scratch—she dabbed at it with some ferns—isn't deep.

Then she froze, staring, for two brown eyes were fixed on her, staring back, small and low, like a little animal's. Well, she reasoned, a child's.

"Hello?" she called cautiously. She walked toward the eyes and reached out to part the underbrush, but there was a quick rustling sound and whoever belonged to them was gone.

Whoever it is can't be very big, she told herself. I must have been right about children playing at the hut.

She cleaned her sneaker off a bit more—the remaining mud was drying rapidly in the heat—and went on. I bet I scared whoever it was to death, she thought. The abominable swampwoman.

She walked slowly, deciding to give the child—if it was a child—time to warn his or her playmates; she heard more rustling ahead.

But no shouts or giggles.

The underbrush thinned out, and the ground rose; the boards ahead of her were intact and dry. Gillian ran across them easily and came out into the small clearing where the hut stood, ringed with old laurels and one or two hemlocks.

The hut itself was tiny, only one room, dominated by a huge fieldstone fireplace at one end, its only claim to beauty. The outside walls were covered with gray shingles, but many were raggedly broken or missing, so the walls looked more like tattered canvas than wood. One window—open—was set in a crooked frame next to the barn-board door; Gillian knew there were three others out of sight, one in each wall of the nearly square building. A bird's nest was perched over the door; a phoebe's, Gillian guessed.

"Hello?" she called, as she had on the path. But there was no answer; no sound at all, in fact.

She called once more, then a third time, but the silence was thick enough to tell her that if anyone had been there, they had already fled into the woods.

She knocked on the door, just in case she was wrong, waited a moment, and then opened it.

33

The junk she remembered seeing inside last year had been pushed into one corner, and the floor and hearth had been swept. The other three windows, like the one by the door, were open, which must, Gillian decided, be why it doesn't smell bad anymore—and there were signs of someone's having used the fireplace.

Red-and-blue boxes on the rough table that stood by the door caught and held Gillian's eyes—the pasta containers from her mother's kitchen. Nearby was the cocoa, next to the instant coffee and the dog biscuits. There were several cans of dog food, too, cans of soup and hash; two plates, cups, and soup bowls were stacked near the groceries, and a larger bowl, filled with water, was on the floor under the table, with an empty foil pie tin beside it.

The Harrisons' thick brown blanket was folded over a pile of hay near the hearth, with the blue blanket next to it. The towels were in a heap on the broken canvas sling chair that she and Margie had scrounged from the dump years earlier, along with several sweaters Gillian didn't recognize.

Not knowing whether to be angry or frightened, Gillian picked up the sweaters. A couple of them were only a few sizes smaller than her own, but the others were little, obviously for a small child.

Then Gillian saw her diary, on a low table made from a slab of wood laid over four stumps near the back window.

It was open, face down, and she felt herself grow hot with anger and embarrassment.

She picked it up, and read what it was open to:

. . . matter so much which way I really am. What matters is knowing. If I only knew, I'd know what to do with my life, about Suze, and about other people. Until I know, I guess I'm just fit for trees and mountains . . .

There was a soft sound from the door, and Gillian dropped the diary, terrified, incapable of moving while the door slowly opened . . .

And closed just as quickly. She could hear scuffling outside, a quick whisper, and the sound of footsteps running into the woods.

Gillian put the diary back on the table, wrenched the door open, and looked wildly around the clearing. But there was no sign of anyone. A branch swayed slightly and she ran to it, but there was no one there, and a soft breeze had come up, anyway; maybe that had made the branch move.

She went back inside.

This is foolish, she thought. I should leave; get the police; tell Mom and Dad.

It's got to be kids, she said to herself, picturing the eyes in the swamp again—little kids and a dog. They probably wouldn't even understand what they read in the diary.

Would they?

Of course they wouldn't. Not if they really were little.

I'm certainly not going to the police about children, even if they did break in. I'd go to their parents, maybe. But mostly just to them.

It's not nice to steal, she said silently, rehearsing.

35

It's fun to play house, but you have to ask permission to use someone else's stuff, someone's hut, someone's dishes. And stealing food's really bad because you can't give it back once you've eaten it, like you can dishes and blankets. Suppose the people you stole from don't have any money to . . .

Out of the corner of her eye, Gillian saw a soft movement, near the pile of junk.

A mouse, I bet. She turned slowly, but instinct told her whatever was there was far larger than a mouse.

The movement came again and then, on a moth-eaten cushion hidden behind a couple of crumbling cardboard boxes, she saw an undersized, thin, long-haired dog, with a clumsily bandaged paw.

Gillian moved the boxes swiftly aside and knelt by the dog, who wagged a feeble tail. "Easy there," she crooned softly. "Easy, puppy, easy. I won't hurt you."

But the dog didn't seem afraid, just weak.

Is this those kids' idea of a joke, she thought angrily, keeping a hurt dog in here in the dark? Then she remembered the food and the water bowl; whoever it was didn't seem to be neglecting the dog. Maybe it was a stray.

It had no collar.

She held her hand out. The dog sniffed it, then licked it and rubbed its face against it, as if asking to be patted. Gillian ran her hand around to the back of the dog's neck and stroked; there were thick mats behind its ears. "Poor puppy," she said softly. "Poor puppy. No one's brushed you."

Should she take the dog home with her? Take it home and clean it up, advertise for its owner? Get a vet to see to that paw? Dr. Morelli, not far from the

Harrisons' cabin, had taken care of Peter's dog, who'd cut himself badly the summer before.

But what about the kids? Maybe the dog belonged to one of them.

I'll have to find them, she decided, giving the dog a final pat and scrambling to her feet. "You stay right here, good dog," she said. "I'll be right back. Good pup. Want some water?" She moved the water bowl closer. The dog lapped some, but politely, as if it knew that was what Gillian expected.

Gillian went outside—the sunlight made her eyes ache after so long in the dim hut—and walked around the clearing, peering into the woods. Again there was no sign of anyone, but she was sure she was being watched, so she went back to the hut, stood by the front door, and said loudly, "I won't hurt you. Hey, come on, I know you're here. I found your dog, and it looks sick. I think it ought to go to a vet. May I take it to one? I won't tell anyone about the things you stole. But you shouldn't have stolen them. Come on, kids, I won't hurt you. I won't tell."

She paused. Nothing.

"I'm taking the dog, then. To the vet." She hesitated. She should tell them where she lived, but that would mean they'd know the diary was hers.

Well, no. Other people could live in the same house.

Should she say she was taking the diary back?

But that would be admitting that it was hers.

"I live in the house at the end of the path, the swampy one. You can come anytime for the dog."

She went back into the hut when there was no answer.

Just as she was coming out again, the dog in her

37

arms and the diary in one hand, a little blond boy of about five appeared at the edge of the clearing, his face filthy, his jeans torn, and his brown eyes unmistakably the ones that had looked out at Gillian in the swamp.

"My dog," he said. "Don't take her."

Five

BEHIND HIM STOOD a girl, by appearance his much
older sister—probably a few years younger than Gillian, though. Eyes as huge as the boy's, but sadder,
regarded Gillian warily from a pale heart-shaped face
framed by stringy shoulder-length brown hair. The
girl put one hand protectively on the boy's shoulder;
the cuffs of her long-sleeved shirt were, Gillian noticed, frayed, and the shirt itself was far too big for
her. It hung baggily below her knees and flapped
against her jeans when she moved.

"My dog," said the boy again. "We found her. Her
name's Lady."

"Okay." As soon as Gillian put her down, Lady
walked shakily to the children and lay on the ground
near them. Gillian's eyes, though, remained on the
girl. Was she, then, the thief? "But Lady needs to go
to a vet."

The girl spoke at last, in a soft, surprisingly gentle voice, apologetic, and weak, as if there were very little breath, or perhaps conviction, supporting it. "I know," she said. "But I can't take her."

"Why not?" Gillian asked.

The girl smiled; it was a scared child's smile, wan and tremulous. "I don't know a vet. I don't have any money." Her eyes fell to the diary, which Gillian still held, and widened.

"Yes, it's mine," Gillian said belligerently. "And the hut and half the stuff you've got inside belong to my folks. The Harrisons. I'm Gillian. Are you sure you didn't steal Lady, too?"

The moment she'd said that, she wished she could take it back, for the girl's huge eyes filled with tears and her hand tightened on the boy's shoulder. She didn't speak.

"If you stole the dog," Gillian said less harshly, "someone's bound to be looking for her. And she's bound to be unhappy, missing her owners."

"We found her!" said the boy loudly. "We didn't take her. Don't you be mean to Lark."

"Lark?" Gillian stepped closer to them; the girl had turned away, her face hidden behind her hair. How long, Gillian wondered, has it been since she combed it?

"My sister," said the boy protectively, putting his thin arm around Lark's knees and twisting his head around to face Gillian. "Don't you hurt her."

"I'm sorry I took it," said Lark defensively. "The diary. I bumped into the picture and found it. But I didn't read much. It's only . . ."

"Only what?" asked Gillian more sharply than she intended. She didn't know which embarrassed her more, the thought of Lark's reading the diary or of Lark's seeing how she felt about her reading it.

"Only," Lark whispered, "that it helped. I'm sorry about the other stuff, too. Go ahead and take it back. Just leave us alone, okay?"

But how could she?

"The other stuff isn't all ours." Gillian jammed the diary into her pocket. "The police said someone had been breaking into cabins."

"So what?" said the boy fiercely, clinging to Lark. "They don't need it. We need it, Lark says, we . . ."

"Jackie," Lark warned, and the boy immediately fell silent.

"Are you runaways?" Gillian asked, gently this time.

"No!" Jackie shouted, then added, as if he'd rehearsed it, "We're camping. Playing. Mommy lets us."

Gillian could feel both of them studying her face, as if testing the effect of their obviously manufactured story, and deliberately, she sat down on the stoop. "It's okay," she said. "I won't tell." But she knew she should, probably. They were both grimy and ragged; they looked hungry—and worse, miserable and frightened.

"The stuff doesn't matter," she said carefully. "You didn't take anything really good. Except the big blanket."

"Take it back." Lark nearly knocked Gillian over, darting past her into the hut and coming out again with the blanket bundled in her arms, thrusting it at her. "Here. Just go away. Please." She dropped her eyes as if to soften the urgency in her voice. "Please go away. Please leave us alone."

41

Gillian stood up, ignoring the blanket. "But you don't have much food; you need—cots, I don't know. The hut's a mess. At least let me help you clean it up. You cleaned it some, I know, but . . ." She stopped, startled at her offer.

Lark let the blanket fall to the ground. "Please," she whispered, taking Gillian's hand. Her own was small and fragile, the veins blue under the thin white skin. She must have two shirts on, Gillian realized, seeing the edge of something white under her cuff; in this heat?

"Well," Gillian said awkwardly; Lark was still clinging to her hand, and Jackie was standing near the stoop, both arms around the dog. "Let me get help for the dog at least. I do know a vet. Let me take her."

"No." Lark dropped Gillian's hand and went down the stoop, to Jackie. "No, he'll ask; you'll have to tell."

"She'll ask," Gillian corrected. "The vet's a woman. And I'll say I found the dog. I did, sort of."

Lark turned away. "Keep her if you want," she said in a hollow voice, suddenly devoid of emotion.

"Lark!" Jackie protested. "No!"

"It's better, Jackie," said Lark emptily. "We can't feed her. Suppose someone comes and she barks? And when we leave . . ."

"No. I'll go home," he said stubbornly. "I'll tell."

"No, Jackie. No." Lark put her hands on her brother's shoulders. "You won't tell," she said, her eyes boring into his. "Hush about that. You know you don't want to go back. You know what will happen if you do. Let her take Lady. She seems nice."

"No." Jackie was in tears now. "No."

"Jackie," said Gillian helplessly, going to them. "Look. I'll just take her to the vet. I'll bring her back

42

here afterward." She turned to Lark. "I could bring more food for her, so you'll have it for later. Maybe bring you some, too . . ." What am I saying, she wondered.

But what horror had they come from? It was pretty obvious they hadn't run away for the fun of it.

Lark regarded her suspiciously; Gillian tried to tell her with her eyes that she wouldn't betray her.

But mightn't I?

Not till I know what's wrong, she decided.

"Please," she said to Lark. "I like animals. I know how Jackie feels. And you. I think you like—Lady, too."

Lark nodded, but the gesture seemed empty again, as if she'd suppressed whatever liking she had as soon as it appeared the dog could be better tended elsewhere.

"That's settled, then," said Gillian. "Okay. Can I take Lady now?"

Jackie nodded, and he and Lark watched while Gillian bent down in front of Lady, who was still lying near them.

"Hi, Lady." Gillian held out her hand, and the feeble tail beat against the ground. "Want to come with me, girl? Just for a while. Dr. Morelli won't hurt you; she loves dogs. She'll want to help you. Come on, girl, come on." Gillian straightened, slapping her thigh, and the dog struggled to her feet, holding up her hurt paw. Gillian could see the shape of bones beneath her matted coat.

"You prob'ly better pick her up," Jackie said. "She might fall down."

Gillian nodded; she'd already noticed that the dog had stumbled when she'd tried to walk.

Jackie ran to Lady, steadying her. "You'll bring her back?" he asked anxiously. "We could still keep her?"

"I'll bring her back," Gillian told him. "I promise." She reached out and tousled Jackie's hair. "I wouldn't separate a boy and his dog."

"Lark likes Lady, too," he said loyally. "She just can't say about liking sometimes. She . . ."

"Jackie," warned Lark. "Remember."

"But you said she's nice," Jackie whispered, glancing longingly at Gillian.

Lark almost smiled. "Yes. She's nice." Then she did smile, at Gillian, although faintly. "Thank you. Thank you, *Gillian*." She said the name carefully, as if to register it in her memory.

"You're welcome," Gillian answered, relieved. "I'll bring Lady back soon. It might not be today, okay? The vet might want to keep her overnight or something. But it'll be soon."

"And you won't . . ."

"I won't tell where you are. I won't say anything about you. I'll say I found the dog in the woods, on the dirt road, maybe, near our place, wandering. Or I'll just say I found her and leave it at that. Do you," she asked awkwardly, "need anything? I mean," she added, realizing they needed nearly everything, "anything in particular?"

"No," Lark said, looking away.

"Sure?"

"Come in, Jackie," Lark said evasively. "Time to go in!" She pushed him ahead of her into the hut, and shut the door.

It took Gillian nearly three times longer than usual to cross the swamp, but Lady managed to stay upright, with occasional stops and many pats from Gillian. She seemed a plucky dog, part golden retriever perhaps, but surely not all golden, for her muzzle was too pointed, her head too narrow, and her coat was marked with occasional faint dabs of white and black. Part collie, along with the golden? Whatever she was, she was friendly and brave, and Gillian lost her heart to her quickly.

Luckily, no one seemed to be around when she got home. She boosted Lady into the back of the Toyota, opened the windows partway to keep the car as cool as possible, and went cautiously into the kitchen, where she found a note:

M and P out in boat; Mom at farm for strawberries; Dad working.

Gillian scrawled:

G to village.

at the bottom, deciding that was close enough to the truth; she didn't want to say anything about Lady till she was surer of what to do about the kids.

She ran up to her room, put the diary back behind the picture, and then hurried out to Lady, who was lying quietly in the back seat. She knew Dr. Morelli would prefer to be telephoned first, but she also decided her story might seem truer if she didn't do that; she drove straight there.

There were several people and animals ahead of her in the waiting room—dogs, cats, a rabbit—but the receptionist clucked her tongue over Lady's thinness and said of course Dr. Morelli would squeeze her in. Lady curled up obediently at Gillian's feet while they waited, as if grateful to be on the soft carpet and in front of the large floor fan.

At last it was their turn, and Dr. Morelli, who didn't look much older than Margie, smiled warmly when Gillian led Lady into the examining room. Dr. Morelli's hands were so large they appeared clumsy, but Gillian had never seen them falter on an animal's body, or move with anything but gentle kindness— reverence, it almost seemed—for the life in her care. "Nice to see you, Gillian," she said. "How's that dog of your sister's?"

"Her boyfriend's, actually. Fine, I think. Peter's here for the summer, but he and Margie will be down in South County doing summer stock, which means they'll be pretty busy, so Peter decided to leave the dog with his parents. We still have biscuits left over from his visit last summer, though." Then she remembered they didn't, and changed the subject to Lady quickly; Dr. Morelli had already let the dog sniff her hand, and was scratching her ears. "I found her near our place," Gillian said. "Someone's bandaged her paw, but she looks awfully thin."

Dr. Morelli palpated Lady's body expertly; Lady licked her hand when it came near her head. "Half starved." Dr. Morelli's voice barely hid her anger. "And coming back—not fast enough—from dehydration. My guess is that someone abandoned her; she's friendly enough to have been a pet for a while, but she's pretty young, I'd say. No sign of a collar when you found her, right?"

"Right."

Dr. Morelli prodded a bit more, looked into Lady's

mouth and ears, took her temperature, and held a stethoscope against her. "She'll need special food for a while, Gillian; it may be expensive."

Gillian tried not to gulp; she'd saved quite a bit of money for college, and had transferred her account to Pookatasset, because she was planning to leave directly from there after she and Suzanne had taken a goodbye trip to Cape Cod at the end of August. But she hadn't planned to use the money for much besides college and the trip; she'd hoped to take most of it to Oregon.

"Are you prepared to look after her?" Dr. Morelli asked, cutting the filthy bandage off Lady's paw, which Lady obligingly held up. "I know your folks have said they don't want a dog in the city."

"I thought I might take her to Oregon State," Gillian said, making that up quickly, "if no one claims her. I'm going there in the fall. I think I might be able to get permission to keep a dog. If I can't, I could try to find someone around here to keep her. I can't just let her go."

"No, you can't. Umm—this looks a bit nasty."

The paw had been badly cut, and it was so scabbed over with blood and pus that it was hard to see the extent of the wound.

"Tell you what," said Dr. Morelli. "You leave her with me overnight, okay? That way, I can fix up her paw, get some fluids into her, and start her on some vitamins and special food."

"Okay, but how much . . ."

"No charge." Dr. Morelli patted Lady's flank. "You're a good Samaritan, the way I see it, and you're going to have enough expenses ahead of you as it is. I'll charge you for her care after this visit, but—she's a sweetheart, isn't she?" Lady had licked Dr. Morelli's face. "And grateful to be looked after. Any ideas for a name, by the way?"

"Um—no. Lady, I guess."

"As good as any." Dr. Morelli hugged the dog. "You're a lucky lady, Lady," she said, opening the door to the inner surgery. "Frank! Admission!"

She turned back to Gillian. "You get her a collar and leash, and see the town clerk about a license. She hasn't been spayed; the clerk will ask that. You can always cancel the license if her owner turns up and she has one. Or transfer it if you give her to someone else. Get some of this at the feed store in the village, too." She wrote something on a small pad and tore the sheet off, handing it to Gillian. "Keep her on it— it's extra-nourishing, easy-to-digest food—for five days or so. Then start her on regular food. If she gets sick, put her back on the special stuff for a while and let me know. Okay?"

"Yes."

"You should put an ad in the local paper," Dr. Morelli went on, "and notices in a couple of stores. What's the matter?"

Gillian thought quickly. "It's just—well, we're trying to keep the phone line sort of free," she said lamely. "Dad's expecting an important call. Could I put your number in the ad? I'll check in with you, and . . ."

"You're a bad liar, Gillian," said Dr. Morelli, laughing. "Sure, use my number. I doubt anyone'll turn up, anyway. But look, given your—er—hesitation, you'd really better talk to someone about keeping Lady."

"I will," Gillian said.

"And she should be spayed, when she's stronger,

unless whoever ends up with her wants puppies." Dr. Morelli smiled. "You did the right thing, Gillian. She's a wonderful dog. Don't worry; I won't interfere with the logistics. All I care about is that she finds a home. She'll be a good friend to you, or to whoever keeps her."

She probably will, Gillian thought, backing the Toyota out of the lot and heading for the village and the town clerk's office. But will Lark and Jackie be able to be good friends to her?

Six

BRAD WAS AT THE Finnegans' farm stand with his sister when Gillian drove by on her way to the village. He flagged her down and she thought of telling him about Lady—even asking him if he might want her—but again she decided it might be better not to mention her till she'd figured out what to do about Lark and Jackie.

It would be hard, though, not to tell him the whole story.

I could just ignore him, she thought.

But he'd stepped into the middle of the road and was holding up his thumb.

"Blast it," Gillian muttered, pulling over.

"Ride to town, lady?" Brad asked, sliding in.

"My mother always told me not to talk to strangers," she said primly, starting up again.

"Mine, too." He settled back as if she picked him up every day at this time. "Morning. Hot, isn't it?"

"Umm-hmm. Morning."

"Where are we off to?"

"Oh," she said vaguely, "just some errands. Stuff for Mom. You?"

"Oh, just some errands. Stuff for your mom. So where's the first stop?"

She tried to swallow her annoyance; it wasn't his fault the situation was awkward—and she'd made it so herself, by deciding not to tell him about the dog. "Grocery store," she said, wishing she'd noticed her mother's shopping list before she'd left. But she could always get things to go with the strawberries—short-cake makings. And then drive back and get the dog supplies later. Go to the newspaper office then, too, and the town clerk.

"Movies tonight?" Brad asked after a few minutes' silence. "There's a good one, one of those old swash-bucklers we used to laugh at. And the theater's air-conditioned."

Gillian pulled into the parking lot of Pookatasset's small supermarket. "How about Michelle?"

"She's away with her family. Poconos. Once again: movie?"

"Okay," she said unenthusiastically, shutting off the ignition.

"Hey, black eyes." Brad put a finger under her chin and lifted it; she'd never liked that gesture of his and it irritated her doubly now. "You all right? You seem down. Got a problem I should know about? Tell Uncle B."

That freed her, at least. She gave a snort, said, "No!"

51

and got out of the car, striding briskly into the store.

She bought a pint of whipping cream, a box of biscuit mix, and a half gallon of milk. All those things would do for the shortcake, and they could always use the remaining milk, especially with Margie and Peter there for a few days, and Suzanne coming.

On the way out, Brad stopped at the bulletin board in the supermarket's entry. "Hey, Gill," he said. "Look. They've been doing this for a month or so. You have anything like it in New York? It gives me the creeps, but I guess it's a good idea."

Gillian turned back and looked where he was pointing.

A line of photographs marched across the top of the bulletin board that ran the length of the entryway. "MISSING," said the caption in huge black letters. The photos beneath it were all of children and teenagers, with statistics under each one: age, height, weight, address, when and where last seen . . .

Gillian found herself staring into Jackie's eyes, and next to him was Lark.

"Lark Jenkins," it said under her picture. "Age 14. Height 5'½". Weight 92 lbs. 111 Claymore Road, Providence. Last seen, June 3 . . ."

". . . can't figure out where they all go," Brad was saying.

"Wh—what?"

"I said I can't figure out where they all go. You must get even more of them in the city. The store here just does Rhode Island kids; I guess they're trying to supplement those milk-carton pictures. Somehow, the kids on those all seem to be from Texas or California. I wonder if runaways really go that far. Gillian?"

"Huh?"

"What's the matter?"

"Oh—nothing. The pictures give me the creeps, too." She held the door open. "Yes, we have them in New York. I never noticed them much, though. New York's full of runaway kids, I guess. Come on, let's go."

He gave her a look, but followed silently till they were in the car again, and then he said, "Did you ever think of running away? I mean, when you were a kid?"

"Me? No, never." She backed the car out of its space.

"I did. When I was around six. I packed up a little suitcase, the kind people take on airplanes. Pajamas, underwear, toothpaste, toothbrush, corn flakes, clean shirt, teddy bear . . ."

She couldn't help laughing. "Toothpaste and teddy bear and corn flakes!"

He laughed, too. "Yup. And I walked all the way to Route 102, and then I sat down and didn't know where to go next, so I went back home again and unpacked."

"Why'd you do it?" she asked curiously. "I mean, why did you want to run away?"

"You know, I don't even remember. Might have been a fight with Dad; he was always yelling at me back then. He didn't so much after that, though, so Mom must've figured out that I'd tried to run away, and said something to him. But I think I also just wanted to see what it was like. Hey, you drove past the farm!"

Gillian gritted her teeth. "Sorry." She went on till she found a driveway to turn in.

"I've got a slow day," Brad remarked on the way

back. "Too late for planting most things and too early for much harvesting, and my sister's doing farm-stand duty. How about we fix a picnic, go out in one of the boats . . ."

"I can't, Brad," Gillian told him, stopping in front of the stand. "I've got lots of stuff to do. I'll see you tonight, okay?"

"What stuff, Gillian? Come on, can't . . ."

"Brad," she said firmly, "I'll see you tonight."

"Okay, okay. You can't blame a guy for trying."

Can't I just, thought Gillian, slamming her foot down on the accelerator as soon as he'd gotten out, and, in case he was watching, speeding down a side road that would take her back to the village a different way.

Gillian, you're not being fair, she said to herself when she'd cooled down a bit. He's not clairvoyant.

She bought a red nylon collar that looked the right size, and a red nylon leash to match, then two red plastic dishes, one for water and one for food. "Red's her color," she thought of saying to Lark and Jackie, to make them laugh, maybe. "Lady told me to buy everything red." She got a brush, too, and resisted a rawhide bone, but she did buy a big box of dog biscuits.

On the way out of the supermarket, she stood in front of the posters again, looking at Lark and Jackie.

They must have left together—well, of course. Had she taken him against his will, or had he wanted to go? If Lark had taken him, could she get into legal trouble for it, as well as for stealing and breaking into houses?

Could she, Gillian, get into trouble for helping them?

Gillian drove slowly to the town clerk's office for the license, and as she put her own name on the form and handed the clerk the fee, she wondered if she was getting in more deeply than she should, or wanted to. But what was the alternative? Breaking a promise she'd made to a friend—to two friends?

They're not friends, though, she thought, driving to the feed store to pick up the special food. Not yet, anyway.

When she'd gotten the food, Gillian stopped at the newspaper office and wrote out a FOUND ad, giving Dr. Morelli's name and number. She bought some 3 × 5 cards, made a couple of notices, and put one up in the post office and the other in the supermarket. And she almost stopped at the police station to see if anyone had reported a lost dog, then realized that was risky and decided to call anonymously from a phone booth instead. No one had reported one.

When Gillian got home, there was a letter from Suzanne propped up on the kitchen counter next to a revised note about where everyone was. Margie and Peter had picked up the mail, it said, and driven to the theater. Dad was still working, and Mom was up in the field, painting; the berries had been washed and sugared and were in a bowl on the kitchen counter, rendering their juice.

Gillian scrawled "No one buy cream or biscuit stuff; I did" at the bottom of the note, put the groceries away, and hid the dog things in her room. Then she took Suzanne's letter out to the porch to read.

Hi, love,

I know you haven't even left yet, but I don't have anything in particular to do now except go to sleep, and I wanted you to have a letter right after you got to Pookatasset. I've been working on that big cityscape all night and I still can't get it right. There's something wrong with the light in it; I wish I could bring it when I come and ask your mom about it. Even though she always says she's just an amateur, she really knows her stuff.

I miss you.

That creep Richard called. Well, I guess he's not a creep, but he wanted me to go out with him. I wish he'd stop asking me. But if I told him about us, he'd probably blab it to everyone we know, and I don't think I'm ready for that. So I just said the usual stuff about not seeing anyone right now, working hard, etc., etc. I don't think he believed me.

Speaking of Richard, how's Brad? (Not that he's a creep.) I bet you'll have seen him by the time you read this. Is he still the same sweet person? Did you tell him yet? I admire you for doing that, and I know it's tough, but I guess you're right that you have to, that it wouldn't be fair not to. I hope he was okay about it, or will be when you tell him.

And how's Margie and Peter? I wish our lives could be as simple as theirs. But maybe theirs aren't as simple as they seem.

I guess I'm depressed; I'm sorry. It's just that I miss you so much, and we won't really be able to see each other alone much on the Fourth, and it's forever till the end of August when we—HOORAY!—go to the Cape. I don't think I'll believe that till we get off the bus and go to that bike-renting place and ride out to the beach and that cabin. A whole week, just us! And then . . .

But we have to do it; we're right, aren't we? If either of us threw everything over and didn't go to forestry/art school, we'd end up resenting each other and blaming each other and God knows what, and it would be terrible and we'd probably break up. And we can't very well crawl into a hole with each other and pull it in behind us, even though that sounds pretty nice right now; we have to live in the real world, like you said. We're being so blasted adult about it, though, I could barf.

When I think that you haven't even left yet and that I could call you up right this very minute and it wouldn't even be a toll call, my whole hand tingles wanting to reach for the phone. But it's 3 a.m. and I have a funny feeling your folks might be ALARMED. *So I won't.*

What do you think we'll be like when we're 30? Let's see. I'll be a Great Artist, with galleries full of my stuff, and I'll wear a purple beret and a lavender smock and those funny soft shoes your sister says everyone wears in Shakespeare plays. And you'll be a forest ranger in a green uniform (you know you look great in green—good thing, huh?), and we'll live in this little cabin at the edge of the woods someplace, and every morning you'll go off to keep bears away from tourists and I'll go up on some mountain or something and paint. And Margie and Peter will come to visit us, and you'll have told them about us and they won't mind and maybe they'll be married with a whole bunch of kids who'll call both of us Aunt. And our parents will come on

Thanksgiving but we'll keep Christmas for ourselves and our two dogs and three cats and whatever poor creatures you've saved from traps and things.

Maybe someday we'll even know other gay people. Only it all seems like such a long time from now. Mostly I want to feel your arms around me.

But enough. I better not think about that too much. I'm not really as depressed as I sound. At least, I don't think I am.

How are you? How's the lake? Is Sprite *okay? Have you had any adventures yet? Somehow, you always do when you're there.*

Mom said, by the way, that she wishes I'd stay around here for the Fourth of July sometime but I said my going to your cabin is a Tradition and that I'm not about to change it, because it'd be bad luck. Besides, I'd much rather see that cute little parade in Pookatasset than the great big pretentious one my folks go to out on Long Island that they think is "quaint." Ha! They wouldn't know quaint if it walked up to them and asked them to dance.

Oh, I can't wait! Will there be fireworks this year?

Anyway, I'll see you Friday and I don't have to go back till Monday morning. Two whole days, and parts of two others! Wish it were longer.

But it will be. Someday it'll be forever, won't it?

> *All my love,*
> *Suze*

Gillian put the letter in her pocket just as her father came out of his study, his eyes glazed as they often were when he'd been working. He taught sociology at New York University and had been working on a book all year; he hoped to finish it this summer, but Gillian could see right away that it wasn't going well.

"There you are," he said, sitting heavily down in one of the green wooden porch chairs. "I saw you got a letter from Suze. She's still coming for the Fourth, I hope?"

"Yes. She's sort of depressed, but okay."

"Oh?"

"Painting, I guess. Boys. You know Suze."

Her father smiled. "Speaking of boys," he said, "if you want to invite Brad over for dinner sometime, you know it's okay. We can stretch almost any meal for one more person."

"Thanks." Gillian got up restlessly. "How's the book?" she asked, going to the edge of the porch and looking out through the screen at the lake. It was nearly lunchtime, but she didn't feel in the least hungry.

"So-so. You know I can't really talk about it while I'm doing it."

"I wish I had a project like that. Or like Mom's and Suze's painting."

"No, you don't. Not like my book, anyway. Besides, what about all those things you were going to do around the grounds this summer? And how about reading? I'm not sure they're too strong on that in forestry school; besides, no one in college ever has much time for extracurricular reading. Now's the time to do it—nice quiet house, weather too hot to do anything active. Why don't you take *Sprite* and a book and go out to the middle of the lake? Get a nice tan that way, too."

"You think of everything," said Gillian fondly, feeling how different her world was from his, but loving him anyway, and the fact that they'd always been friends. She kissed the top of her father's head; it smelled faintly of his shampoo, a nice, fresh smell. "Thanks, Dad."

Seven

"I WONDER," said Mrs. Harrison at dinner, passing a serving dish of green beans, "if whoever broke into our cabin and the other cabins around here could've been runaways. There's a whole wall of runaway posters up at the supermarket. I guess that's what made me think of it."

Gillian took some beans.

"If I were a runaway," her mother continued, "that's the kind of thing I'd take. Household things."

"If you had a house to put them in," said Margie. "Don't runaways live on the streets?"

"And in cities," said Peter. "They gravitate to cities, don't they? There's more opportunity for them to find food and get work—whatever work they do."

"Sell themselves," said Margie grimly. "No thanks, Gill, no beans."

"Beans," said the professor, taking the dish and putting some on Margie's plate, "are nutritious and not fattening. I don't want an anorexic daughter."

"Dad!" Margie protested.

"Alex, she's an adult," Mrs. Harrison said softly.

"S'okay, Professor Harrison," said Peter, as if trying to steer them away from an argument that would embarrass them all. "She's got to watch her weight for the parts she's playing this summer. But I won't let her starve."

"Beans aren't fattening," the professor said again.

"I don't like beans, Dad," said Margie. "Maybe you've forgotten."

"Oh, my." Gillian rolled her eyes. "The famous bean casserole."

Professor Harrison looked blank for a moment, then groaned. "How could I forget?" A few years earlier they'd had a vegetarian supper whose main dish was a bean casserole made with yogurt, and Margie had refused to eat it. The argument had gotten so fierce that Margie had turned her plate—food and all—upside down on the table and stormed out of the room.

"If anyone in this family," said Margie severely, "tells Peter about that—that episode—I'll never speak to him or her again."

Peter looked around the table, mock-mystified, and everyone laughed.

"What time's your date with Brad, Gillie?" asked Mrs. Harrison, and the subjects of food and runaways were both safely dropped.

The movie was only fair. Gillian's mind kept wandering back to the hut and the supermarket posters. Part of her wanted to confide in someone—her parents, Margie, Peter; maybe Brad; certainly Suze. But

62

the other part was still afraid of betraying Lark and Jackie. It wasn't just that she'd promised not to, or that she'd sensed reporting them would somehow be wrong. Suppose what they'd run from was horrible?

How long could two kids hide out in a primitive hut? And how long could they depend on stealing without getting caught? She couldn't support them, not for long, anyway, if she expected to keep her college bank account intact. As it was, she'd spent quite a lot on Lady, but luckily the next day was Wednesday, when she got the allowance her parents still gave her for doing her share of the household chores . . .

"Where *are* you, Gillian?" Brad asked as they walked to his car. "I just asked what you thought of the fight scene and you were a million miles away."

"Sorry," said Gillian. "The fight scene. You mean the one on the quarterdeck or the one in the castle?"

He gave her a look. "There was no fight on the quarterdeck. The one in the castle."

"Right. The one in the castle." Gillian didn't remember it at all. "I think it lacked a certain technical proficiency, but it more than made up for that in enthusiasm and—er—panache."

"Panache?"

"Panache."

Brad unlocked the driver's door, piloted Gillian around to the other side, unlocked that door, and held it open for her. "I bet you don't know what that means."

"I bet I don't either," she said, trying not to be annoyed at his gallantry, "but it sounded good. I think it fits okay. I mean, I think it's what I mean. Flair, sort of."

Brad got into his side. "Walking dictionary, you are," he said. "How about a Coke?"

"No, I don't think so. Thanks. I'm kind of tired."

"A drive, then?" he suggested. "It's only ten."

"Yes, I know. I'd rather not. Besides, what would Michelle say?"

Brad smiled vaguely. "Hey, you and I are just friends, remember? Michelle doesn't enter into it."

"Sorry."

"Home then, right?"

"Please."

Hi, Suze,

she wrote, once she was safely in her room,

> *This might be a letter I don't dare send, because I'm not sure if I should tell anyone about what I'm going to say in it. But, Suze, I've got to talk to someone. A couple of kids—runaways—broke into our cabin, and now they're living in the hut. I haven't told anyone about them, and now I seem to be trying to help them. They're—I don't know— troubled? There's something sort of desperate about them. There are posters about runaways up in the supermarket, and these kids are on them; I probably should turn them in, but for some reason I'm afraid if I do, something awful might happen.*
>
> *Am I crazy? I wish you were here and we could talk about it. I wish you could do whatever it is I'm doing with me . . .*

But she's not here, Gillian said to herself angrily, tearing up the letter and throwing it away. And even if she were, should you really involve anyone else in this? Suppose helping runaways is illegal?

She took a fresh sheet of paper and wrote:

Hi, Suze, love,

Got your letter and this can't be a long one. "Got your letter" is an understatement—I loved your letter. I miss you, too, horribly, and I know the Fourth is going to be tough on both of us. But at least we can see each other. I can't tell you how much I want to be on the Cape with you right now, just us. Like you, I can't let myself think about it much.

Things here are okay. Yes, Brad's still the same sweet person. And yes, I told him. He took it sort of all right, but I think he's upset. Not disapproving, at least he hasn't said anything rotten about my— our—being gay and our being lovers and all—but I think he's still sort of hung up on me. Maybe he and Richard should get together. (Bad joke.) I think he's hurt, and I wish his girlfriend would come back from the Poconos where she's with her parents. Michelle, her name is. She's a new girlfriend.

You asked about adventures. I've sort of had one and I want to tell you about it, but I'm not sure I can, at least not yet. Okay? I'm sorry. I don't like not telling you things.

Anyway, you were wonderful to send a letter. I don't know if you'll get this before you come. I'd splurge and send it express mail, but I don't think I can afford that.

I love you. Always. You're the one sure thing in my life right now—you and Oregon, but even though I know it's important for me to go there,

and even though I'm looking forward to it, I'll take
you instead of it any day. You know that, right?
                              All my love,
                              Gillie

It was past four when Gillian finally fell asleep.

Eight

"HI, JACKIE."

The little boy regarded Gillian warily when she emerged from the swamp early the next morning, after picking Lady up from the vet and mailing her letter to Suzanne. Jackie's face soon brightened, though, and he ran to Lady and hugged her.

"Lady's going to be just fine," said Gillian, watching him as she put down the bag of supplies. "The vet says she needs special food. I got you a brush. Will you brush her?"

Jackie nodded. "Want to keep her," he said, his face hidden in Lady's long hair.

"I know. We'll have to make sure no one else owns her. And that it's okay with Lark."

"Lark's not my mommy," Jackie said defiantly.

"Where is your mommy, Jackie?"

"Home."

"How come you left?" Gillian squatted down on a

67

dry spot at the edge of the path. "Did someone take you away?"

"Lark," said Jackie, apparently unconcerned.

"Don't you miss your mommy?"

Jackie shook his head, still buried in the dog's hair. Lady twisted around to lick him.

"So you don't want to go home. To Mommy and Daddy. Or do you?"

"Want to stay with Lark," said Jackie. "Daddy's bad. He hit me. I want to stay with Lark."

Gillian pushed herself up. "Daddy hit you? Where?"

Jackie lifted his grimy T-shirt and twisted around so his back was facing Gillian. A large red welt, healing but still inflamed, ran diagonally from his shoulder to his waist. A few smaller welts radiated out from it.

"Dear God," said Gillian under her breath. "Does it hurt?" she asked Jackie, gently helping him pull his shirt back down; she was so angry her hands were shaking.

"Some," he said. "Daddy hit Larkie, too."

"Where is Lark?" asked Gillian, her voice shaking along with her hands. She struggled for control. "I think I'd better talk to her."

Jackie held his hand out to Gillian; Gillian took it and picked up the bag. Entwining his other hand firmly in Lady's coat, Jackie led her across the clearing to the hut.

Lark was outside on the front stoop, bent over a large paper—a road map, Gillian saw as she approached. The big shirt was open today, both front and cuffs, revealing a faded red T-shirt.

"Look," Jackie called as they came closer. "Larkie, look! Lady!"

Lark raised her head, gave Gillian a surprisingly bright smile, and said, "Hey, Jackie, that's great." Lady's tail wagged swiftly, and Lark held out a hand to her; the dog nuzzled it briefly. Lady was steadier now; she'd managed much better on the swamp path, and Gillian had noticed that she wasn't much bothered by her freshly bandaged paw.

But Lady didn't seem the issue now. Still, it was going to be hard to broach the more important subject.

Hedging, Gillian said, "The vet said to feed Lady special food." She put the bag down. "But she also said she'll be okay."

"I can't pay you."

"That's all right. The vet didn't charge."

"What about the food? Where do I get it?"

Gillian pointed to the bag.

"I can't pay you for that, either. And you got other stuff, too."

"Forget it. I had to put up a couple of ads, to see if anyone owns her. But I didn't tell about you and Jackie. The vet doesn't think anyone'll claim Lady."

"Okay," Lark said indifferently, as if dismissing the subject.

Jackie moved off with Lady, after rummaging in the bag and taking out the brush, and Gillian looked down at the map. "How're you doing?" she asked awkwardly.

"All right." Lark folded the map. "It's a long way to New Hampshire."

"That where you're going?"

"Our aunt lives there." Lark tossed her hair back. "I might try to take Jackie to her. I don't know, though."

"How about you?"

Lark laughed, not a happy laugh. "I'm a rolling stone," she said lightly. "I can't stay anywhere. My aunt wouldn't want me, anyway."

Gillian hesitated, then said, "There's pictures up at the supermarket. Runaways. You and Jackie are there."

Lark's expression didn't change. "Yeah? I figured they'd get around to that sooner or later." She laughed again, a short laugh this time. "How'd we look? Were they baby pictures, or what? My folks aren't much for sentimental stuff."

"Pretty good pictures, actually," said Gillian. "I recognized both of you before I read about you."

"What'd they say?"

"Height, weight, address, last seen. Nothing much."

Lark slapped the map against her arm. Her shirt sleeves fell back, and Gillian saw that what she'd thought was the cuff of another long-sleeved shirt was a grimy bandage—gauze and adhesive tape—around her wrist. "Not 'fled intolerable situation'?" Lark said, still lightly. "I read that in the paper once, about some kids."

"No." Gillian tried not to look at the bandage. "Not that." Then she did look at it, deliberately dropping her eyes to it when she saw Lark was watching. "What happened?"

"My cat scratched me. My folks have this real vicious black-and-white cat. Did you know black-and-white cats are mean? Like some people. Take my dad, now."

"Jackie showed me his back," Gillian said, seizing the opportunity. "He said your father also hit you."

"Sure," said Lark, her voice getting strident. "He

70

hits me—and my mother—any time he gets drunk."

"Does he get drunk a lot?"

"Enough. He keeps losing jobs, so then he gets drunk. A social worker came once, and she just said he should go to AA or something like that. My mother wouldn't tell her he hits us sometimes, even though one of the neighbors had called the cops about it, and the cops had called the social worker. At least I guess that's why she came. Someone must've called someone. My mother made me shut up when I started to talk to her, though, to the social worker, I mean. But mostly my father just yells, especially at me. Why do I read so much, why can't I dress right, why can't I be his pretty little girl like I was when I was three, why do I spend so much time in my room, why don't I have more friends? Then, when I do have friends, why do I throw myself away on such creeps? He doesn't like anyone, I guess, but especially not me. Whatever I do, I can't win with him. He does the same thing with Jackie. It's like he has a picture in his head of what he wants us to be, and we neither of us fit it."

Lark stuffed the map into her pocket; she pulled her sleeves down over her wrists and buttoned her cuffs.

"Sometimes I think it's my fault," she went on softly, as if to herself. "Maybe I should be more like what he wants, maybe that's a better way to be. I can't even be what I want, though, whatever that is, so how can I be what he wants? Besides, I don't see that there's much to want to be, anyway." She unbuttoned her cuffs again. "It's too hot for this," she said, rolling the sleeves up, exposing the bandage once more. "It's dumb to hide it now that you've seen it."

Gillian nodded. "I don't believe you," she said, "about the cat."

71

"No. No, you probably wouldn't. You're too honest. Like in your diary. You've had bad stuff, too. At least—inside you."

Gillian pushed aside the reference to her diary. "Want to talk about it?" She tipped her head toward the bandage.

"You know, don't you?"

"I don't *know*. But it doesn't take a lot to guess."

"They tell me it's because of sensitivity," Lark said, sounding much older than fourteen. "Caring about things too much." She tossed her hair back again. "You turn on the TV, and when people aren't yelling at each other the way they do in my parents' house, they're killing each other. There are murders all the time and rapes and child abuse and hostages get killed and people die in plane crashes and in earthquakes or because someone goes crazy and starts shooting people in a shopping mall or kids in a school. And people die in wars, and of cancer, or AIDS, or heart attacks, or drugs. You say in your diary that you like trees and that you're going to college to learn how to be a forester. But if the big bomb comes along, the forests will all burn up. So will all the people. One big death party, right?"

"No, not right," said Gillian. "Not a party, anyway. And I hope not right."

Lark gave her an appraising look. "Well, at least you didn't say the bomb's not coming, or that there's no point in worrying about it. That's what everyone else says. Everyone pretends there's no bomb at all, especially now that we like the Russians again, but even so there are always wars, somewhere. I read in school that back during the Vietnam war some kids set fire to themselves, in France, I think it was, and

Buddhist monks did the same thing in Vietnam itself, and they all hoped it would make people realize that the war was terrible. But it didn't. Everyone said wasn't it too bad that people killed themselves about it, but they all went right on having the war, anyway. It's like it doesn't matter when someone dies. Well, if that doesn't matter, why should it matter if a person lives?"

"But it does matter," Gillian said softly. "It does matter, Lark."

"Why?"

"Because—because people care about each other, because people can make a difference, because . . ."

Lark laughed bitterly and tossed her hair back again. "Are you hungry?" she asked abruptly. "We didn't have breakfast yet. Want some food? I sold my watch," she explained, cocking her head as if challenging Gillian to dispute her. "To this creepy old guy in Providence, downtown. He wanted to buy me, and I thought about it, I really did, but what would I do with Jackie while he was screwing me? So I sold him my watch instead. He wasn't too pleased, but he took it." Without changing inflection or tone, she asked, "Want an apple? I found some yesterday; there's an orchard near here. The ones on the trees aren't ripe, but they had some ripe ones at their stand. Big farm, too, lots of stuff in the fields. Want an apple?"

That would be the Finnegans' farm. Gillian wondered how Lark had managed to steal apples—storage apples, they would have to be, from last year. "No thanks," she said.

"I never eat much." Lark stood up. "But I better get one for Jackie."

She disappeared into the hut, and Gillian sat down

on the stoop, watching Jackie but not really seeing him, as he brushed Lady. Am I out of my depth, she wondered again. Could I hurt them even though I'm trying to help?

But she knew she couldn't leave.

"Jackie," Lark called, coming out again. "Here." She threw him an apple with a long, slow, easy underhand.

He caught it, and she clapped. "Yay for Jackie. You can play on my team, kid! The only time my father notices Jackie," she said to Gillian, "is when Jackie makes him mad or when he makes Jackie play ball with him. But then he yells at him that he's not doing it right, and Jackie gets all upset and drops the ball."

She sat down on the stoop beside Gillian, nudging her over. "See? I'm not scared you'll grab me, the way you said in your diary you thought your friend Suzanne would be if she knew how you felt about her."

Gillian forced a smile. "I'm glad. And just for the record, Suzanne does know now how I feel about her, and she feels the same way about me. Also for the record, grabbing you hasn't occurred to me."

"It's okay," Lark said ambiguously. "I don't scare easily. Nothing much scares me anymore, anyway." She looked beyond Jackie into the woods. "I guess I gave myself away. I lied. I did read your diary. A couple of times. Every word."

"I figured."

"It was better than a lot of books. And it made me sort of want to meet the person who wrote it. I mean, you're like me, a little. You think about things, you know? And you're—all fussed, my mother probably would say. At least about that one thing. Or you were when you wrote it in the diary. I guess you're not fussed so much anymore, though, if Suzanne knows and everything. What gets me is that you wanted so much to find out if you were really gay. You know, it's like you wanted to go on fighting."

"You don't?"

Slowly, deliberately, Lark shook her head. She studied Gillian's face. "Why do I think I can trust you?"

"Because of the diary? You know a lot about me. You don't know *me* at all, but you know more *about* me, in a way, than most people. Suzanne hasn't even read my diary. I have to be careful of you, I guess." Gillian smiled. "You could go blab my private life all over town."

"The Problem," Lark said. "Isn't that what you called it? Yeah, maybe I could blackmail you. Take out an ad, like you did about Lady." She tossed her hair again. "Listen, I'm not gay. All right?"

"Sure," said Gillian easily.

"I don't think it matters a whole lot. What one is. I've had a couple of boyfriends. Sort of, anyway. So what, though? It's no big deal." She looked at Gillian curiously. "How about Suzanne? You said she feels the same way."

Gillian hesitated, wondering how much Lark could really understand. But she seemed unshockable, and very grown up, at least about some things. "Suzanne and I love each other," she said finally. "We're lovers. She's coming to visit on Friday, for the Fourth of July weekend. There's a parade . . ."

"Oh, wow," said Lark sarcastically. "I guess I'll have to stick around for that, right?"

"Right." Gillian tapped Lark's wrist lightly. "Did it hurt?" she asked. "Whoops—sorry! Maybe it still does."

"Only a little," said Lark. "Now, I mean. When I cut it, it didn't hurt at all at first. It did later, a lot. It was awful then. But I was numb, sort of, when I did it. I'd thought about it a long time. I used to check every night to make sure there were still razor blades, but I ended up buying some anyway, just to—you know."

Gillian felt herself wince involuntarily.

"I guess maybe it's because razor blades are so sharp that it doesn't hurt at first. Someone told me that once." Lark got up, thrust her hands into her pockets, and paced in front of the stoop—almost, Gillian realized, as if I weren't here. "Still, I only did one wrist. It bled a lot, all over. I don't think I'd like to do it again that way."

"Why would you?" Gillian asked softly. "Why would you do it again?"

"Because," said Lark, her head bowed, "I'm no good at—at anything. No good anyway. And there's no reason not do it." She lifted her head, and the agony in her eyes made Gillian's throat ache. "Don't you see? Your diary sounds like you'd see, at least some of it."

"I do see some of it—of how you feel, I think. But I'm not sure it's right to take your own life. You're assuming that . . ."

"Yes," Lark interrupted without hesitation, "it's right. It's my life, after all. I didn't ask for it; it just happened." Her voice sounded bitter. "One hot night of passion, right? Only I can't see my parents being passionate about each other. Passionately angry, yes, but passionately in love—forget it." She looked straight at Gillian. "I bet there isn't any real love, anyway. I bet love is a lie they tell us. So how can it matter if a person is gay or straight? I know you say

76

you love Suzanne. But I think the biggest lie people tell, even more than how everything will be okay, is probably the one about love."

Gillian wanted to touch her; it seemed the only way to communicate, to ease her pain. But she didn't move. "I don't believe that," she told Lark. "If I did, I'd feel the way you do. I know I would. But I don't believe it. Loving Suzanne and being loved by her is the best thing in my life, in the world. It makes me— joyous, whole, strong." She paused. "You love Jackie, don't you?"

"No," said Lark stubbornly. "I have to take care of him. That's all. I don't really love him. You'll see. You'll find out it's a lie. People don't want to believe it's a lie, so they don't. And they go on living, lying to themselves about love. About other stuff, too, I guess. I don't think I can do that." She eyed Gillian narrowly. "You don't think it's wrong of me to feel that way?"

"I don't agree with you. But I don't think it's wrong of you to feel it. I'm sorry that you do, but how can an honest feeling be wrong? I suppose if it hurts you, hurts other people . . ."

"Suicide," said Lark, "hurts other people. That's what everyone says. But that's only true if other people care about the person who does the suicide."

"Usually someone does care, though." Gillian struggled for words. "Maybe it doesn't seem like they do, and maybe they can't show it very well, but people usually care. I don't know your parents, and your dad sounds pretty bad, but Jackie said he wants to stay with you. I think he loves you, Lark, even if you don't think you love him, and he certainly needs you. So I think it would hurt him if you killed yourself." She

77

paused for a moment. "But I do agree with you that it's your life." Oh, God, Gillian thought; what am I saying? I believe that, sure, but what if it drives her to it, makes her think it's all right—makes it easier? "I'd rather you didn't do it," she said aloud. "Heck, I just met you; you might turn out to be a friend."

Lark looked at her thoughtfully. "I've got to get Jackie away first, anyway."

"New Hampshire's pretty far. And I bet he'll want to stay with you. But shouldn't you talk to someone before you just take him up there? A social worker, maybe?"

"No! Social workers are no good; remember, one came."

"But if you talked to one on your own, without anyone else there, maybe it would be better. Or if you talked to a teacher . . ."

"I can't talk to anyone at school. I don't like the doctor our mother takes us to. And we don't go to church. There. Aren't those all the usual people? Cops? Come on!"

"Cops can be nice, Lark, they really can."

"I've been stealing, remember?"

"Okay." Gillian felt defeated, and she could see that Lark had had enough; she was closed to her now. There had to be something that would ease the tension.

"Hey," Gillian said finally, struggling to sound enthusiastic, "didn't I hear you and Jackie swimming the other night? Want to go for a swim?" Then she wondered if that was wise. But surely no one would think it odd to see kids swimming, and no one would be likely to get close enough to recognize Lark and Jackie from their poster pictures.

Lark stayed still for a minute, then laughed nervously—like a fourteen-year-old again, Gillian thought; she changes so fast!

"Yeah," said Lark. "Yeah, okay. But Jackie and me, we don't have bathing suits. We go in our underwear. Not very modest."

"I might have an extra suit," Gillian said. "An old one, from when I was younger. Not for Jackie, but for you."

"Okay. Jackie doesn't care, anyway."

"Good," Gillian said. "I'll go home and get it. I'll be right back."

Nine

GILLIAN WALKED SLOWLY along the swamp path, still reeling from Lark's words, the reason for her bandage, and the red welts on Jackie's back. Obviously, they needed help, and it didn't look as if they would accept it from the usual channels; Lark wouldn't, anyway. Maybe going to that aunt in New Hampshire would be the best solution. At least Jackie might be safe there, and maybe the aunt could persuade Lark to stay, too.

But it would be hard for them to get there—and maybe the aunt wouldn't want either of them . . .

"There you are!" Margie called as Gillian emerged from the woods and went into the house. "That was a pretty long walk!"

"I guess," Gillian answered with difficulty, feeling as if she'd just entered another world. Had Margie ever seen welts like Jackie's, heard a story like Lark's? "I'm on my way out again," Gillian said, finding nor-

80

malcy, cheerfulness, almost impossible. "Just getting my bathing suit—going swimming."

"Great, I'll go with you. Peter's down at the theater, but I don't have to be there till later. A swim would be terrific."

Gillian stopped on the stairs. Now what?

"Next time," she said. "Okay? I'm going with some kids."

"Anyone I know?"

"Nope."

Margie followed her up to the balcony. "Brad called. He has to work the farm stand this morning, but he said to tell you he'll come over when he takes his lunch break. And Peter and I want to invite you and Brad to go to dinner with us. We've got to move down to the theater soon, and we feel we haven't seen you at all. Gillian, what is it? You're hopping up and down like a six-year-old!"

"I told those kids I'd be right back."

"Friends of Brad's?"

Gillian paused at her bedroom door. "No," she said. "Sorry, Margie, but—a little privacy, okay?" She went into her room and closed the door.

Margie snorted. "I'm your sister!" she shouted. "I changed your diapers."

"You did not!" Gillian shouted back, rummaging in her drawer. Surely she'd kept that old bathing suit; it had been her favorite and she hadn't been able to bear the idea of throwing it away. Yes, there it was. "You were only four." She put the suit on the bed.

"Well, I helped."

"I've grown since then. Maybe you haven't noticed. Matured. Developed."

"Yeah? You're kidding."

"Nope." Gillian struggled out of her clothes and pulled on her current bathing suit, one of the few garments she had that she was vain about. Its deep red made her hair look darker and her eyes brighter, and gave a warm tone to her rapidly tanning dark skin. Maybe Suze liked her in green, but Gillian was pretty sure she'd change her mind when she saw her in this.

"Out of my way, Margie," Gillian said, emerging from her room and running downstairs to the bathroom, hoping Margie wouldn't notice the extra suit bundled under her arm. She wished she could take *Sprite*—rowing might be quicker—but Lark would be listening for her on the path. Still, Margie would be able to guess where she was going if she went on the path; rowing might help disguise it. Even if Margie watched her leave, she could soon be out of sight from the house.

She grabbed a towel from the bathroom shelf—she almost took a couple of extras, but remembered that Lark had already done that—and hastily rolled the extra bathing suit up in it.

Margie stood outside the bathroom, hands on her hips. "You better take a shirt or something," she said. "It may be cooler today, but it's pretty sunny."

"I have dark skin, Mother," said Gillian. "I'm tan already." But she ran back up to her room, took a shirt anyway, and thrust her feet into sneakers.

Margie seized her arm as she went by, nearly dislodging the hidden suit. "Dinner or not dinner?" she asked. "I'd like to make a reservation for, say, seven. Peter and I will be rehearsing down at the theater till five or so. All right?"

"Fine."

"Do you think you could manage to tell Brad?"

"Yes, sure. Margie . . ."

"Okay, okay. Is one of those kids anyone Brad should worry about? Tall, dark, and handsome? Short, cute and scholarly? Medium . . ."

"No, no, and no! Get off my case! You're worse than Mom." Gillian burst out the door and ran down to the lake to launch *Sprite*. I hope Margie *is* watching, she thought. She glanced toward the porch but couldn't make out if any of the shadows up there was Margie or not.

Lady barked as Gillian landed *Sprite* in the little bay near the hut, and by the time she'd pulled the boat up, Lark and Jackie, Jackie clad only in his underpants, were down at the shore, too. "A boat!" squealed Jackie. "Lark, look, a boat! Can I have a ride, Gillie, can I, can I?"

Gillian hesitated momentarily, still worrying about Lark and Jackie's being seen. But it did seem unlikely, even if they went out in *Sprite*. There were no houses nearby, no other boats, either. She could stay close to the shore, and if Lark wanted a boat ride, too, she could always take them to the marsh where the hawk lived; that was almost always deserted.

"Sure, you can have a ride," she said to him. "I'll take Jackie out while you change," she called to Lark, tossing her the bathing suit. "It's clean. Hasn't been worn in years. I hope it fits."

"Thanks."

Gillian reached out to help Jackie, who had waded into the water and was already climbing into the boat. The welts looked even redder in the bright sunlight; she hoped they wouldn't burn.

83

"Come on, Lady," Lark called when Jackie was safely aboard. "You'd better stay inside." She went back up the path, Lady dancing at her heels.

"Can I row, Gillie, can I?" Jackie asked when Gillian had settled him in the stern and had pushed off into deeper water.

"Yup." Gillian helped him move to the middle thwart. "You take one oar, and I'll take the other, okay? That way, I can show you how."

" 'kay." Jackie grasped the oar firmly in both hands, studying the way she did it.

"That's right. Now you put it in the water like this—right—and then you pull back like this. That's all there is to it. In—pull—out. In—pull—out. In—pull—out." She made her strokes short and shallow to match his. "Hey, you're pretty good."

"Let's be pirates," Jackie said, turning to her. "Okay?"

"Okay," said Gillian. "I used to pretend to be pirates myself, with my sister. Only we have to try to be quiet, so no one finds us. Yo-ho-ho and a bottle of rum. Look out, sailors, here we come!"

"Yo-ho-ho and a bottle of *rum!*" Jackie chanted delightedly. "Look out, sailors, here we *come!*" In his excitement, he dipped his oar too shallowly and nearly fell overboard when it skimmed the water's surface. Gillian grabbed him just in time. "Careful, Mate Peg-leg," she said, keeping her voice down to encourage him to, and feeling how small and fragile his body was. "That's called catching a crab. Make sure you put your oar in deeper. Even pirates have to pay attention to what they're doing. Let's try again. Yo-ho-ho . . ."

They'd followed the shoreline for about fifty yards and had turned back again when Lark appeared, waving, in Gillian's old bathing suit. Gillian waved back, and headed Jackie in. Lark looked good in the suit, although it was loose around the top; Lark was thin and still quite small. But she'd knotted the straps in back, which held it up firmly.

As they approached, Lark waded into the water, then did a smooth surface dive and came up beside the boat, resting one hand lightly on the gunwale on Gillian's side.

"Yo-ho-ho," Jackie cried gleefully, "and a bottle of rum. Look out, sailors, here we come! We're pirates," he explained. "We make people walk the plank. Come in this boat and we'll make you do it, won't we, Gillie?"

"Cap'n Blood, you mean," said Gillian, studying Lark's face. She seemed calm, outwardly, anyway. "We sure will, Mate Peg-leg."

Lark pushed down on the gunwale with both hands, nearly swamping them, and flipped herself in. She was more agile than Gillian had expected, and her arm muscles looked stringy but strong under her smooth and very white skin; the wrist bandage was soggy, and filthy in contrast.

"You've gotta walk the plank now," Jackie said. "Doesn't she, Gillie?"

"Sure," Gillian answered, but she wondered, watching Lark closely, if the game was a good idea.

"Yeah!" shouted Jackie. "Yo-ho-ho! You have to jump off, Larkie," he explained patiently. "Please do it. Please play."

For a moment Lark didn't react, but then she stood,

bowed her head contritely, and, like an actress playing Lady Macbeth in the sleepwalking scene, balanced
precariously on the stern thwart.

Gillian watched her anxiously, still wondering if she
should be worried.

But Lark spread her arms wide and, drawing them
into a diving position, said calmly, "You forget, pirates, that some of us can swim." She dove gracefully
in.

When she came up, grabbing on to the side near
Gillian again, she was smiling. "How'd I do?" she
asked.

"Just fine." Gillian held out her hand and helped
her aboard, not wanting to risk another near-swamp-
ing. "Want to row a bit, or swim?"

"Row, row, row!" Jackie said, and so they did, at
first Gillian and Jackie, so Jackie could show off his
new skill to Lark, and then Lark and Jackie, and, when
he finally tired, Lark and Gillian. "I could row by
myself, you know," Gillian said when she and Jackie
exchanged places.

"I know," said Lark. "But it's more fun with two.
And easier."

They fell quickly into each other's rhythm, and
rowed silently; Gillian headed them toward the
marsh.

The hawk was resting on a dead tree as they entered
the narrow channel, and Lark caught her breath when
he rose, spiraling, into the sky. "He's so beautiful,"
she whispered. "He's so free!" Her eyes looked less
haunted—almost happy. "Thank you," she said softly,
"for a nice time."

"Hey," said Gillian, trying to lighten the mood, "it's
not over yet. There's a deserted bridge down here—

the path over it's hardly ever used—and I know a game we could play with Jackie there."

She guided the boat, with Lark still rowing beside her, to where a small wooden bridge spanned the trickle the channel became as it disappeared into the swamp. It was humid and still, almost dark, under the overhanging trees and vines. She welcomed the shadows; both Lark and Jackie showed signs of sunburn, and she'd already made Jackie put on her shirt, even though it was huge on him.

"When I was real little," said Lark, "before Jackie was born, we went to Florida. My parents and me. Things were okay then. Some of Florida was like this. Bigger, though, and scarier. But overgrown."

"It's all the water, I guess," Gillian said, shipping her oar and motioning Lark to do the same; the water was too weedy for rowing. "Makes things flourish. I've always wanted to come here in winter and see it frozen, with snow."

Lark shivered. "Winter," she said, and she seemed to slip away again. She appeared to be watching Jackie, who was leaning over the side, trying to push lily pads and lake weed away from the boat. But Gillian sensed she was removed from both of them in her mind, and from the place.

Gillian lifted her oar and poled the boat to the bridge, where she unclipped the anchor from the bow line and tied *Sprite* to one of the bridge's supports, over on one side, near the shore. "Come on," she said, holding out her arms for Jackie. "Up you go. We've got a game to play."

"You're so good with him," said Lark when they were on the bridge and Gillian had showed Jackie how to race twigs by dropping them in on one side and trying to guess which one would come out first on the other. They all played for a while, and then, leaving Jackie to race against himself, Gillian and Lark sat on a large rock at the other end of the bridge. "I wish you could take Jackie," Lark said as they watched him concentrate intently on his game. "Maybe your parents could adopt him. Wouldn't you like a brother?"

"I'd love Jackie," said Gillian, realizing that she would, "but I'm not sure my folks want another kid. And I don't think anyone can adopt a child who's already got parents. You know, parents who are around to take care of him."

Lark snorted. "I bet my folks wouldn't mind. I bet they don't want either of us back."

"Are you sure?"

Lark picked up a stick and began digging holes in the damp, peaty soil. "Pretty sure. They might want him more than they want me, but I don't think they want either of us much."

"What are you going to do about yourself?" asked Gillian carefully. "If you get Jackie to your aunt's or someplace else, then what?"

"You know."

"You're sure?"

"Pretty sure."

"You had a good time today, though. You even said."

Lark lifted her head, tossing her damp hair back in the gesture Gillian had come to expect. "Having a good time isn't it. It isn't enough."

"Of course not. But doesn't it help?"

"Maybe it helps *you*. You don't have—well, yes, you did have The Problem. Didn't it haunt you, Gillian?

Didn't it follow you all the time, make you feel hollow and scared and lonely inside?"

"For a while. But then I realized I really am gay, and that it's better to live the truth than to live a lie. It doesn't haunt me anymore. I just wish Suzanne and I could be together, and more open about it. But that'll come, I think."

"What if it doesn't? Then what? Wouldn't that be an awful life? Hiding or being cut off from everyone because straight people don't like gay ones? Or are suspicious of them?"

"Yes, maybe, but I don't think it has to be like that. I've read some stuff, and it seems to me gay people can be just as happy as anyone else. I don't see why gay people can't have straight friends as well as gay ones. My friend Brad's straight. You are. You aren't suspicious or hostile, and neither's Brad. I'm not going to expect the worst, Lark. I think that's what you do, though," she added quietly. "Expect the worst."

"Because," said Lark, "that's all there really is. For me, anyway. The worst. Long ago I thought it was just my parents, and that if I got away from them it would be okay. But then I saw all the other stuff, like wars and hostages and how unhappy people are. Like I said, no one really loves anyone; people get divorced all the time, if they have any sense, that is."

"My parents," Gillian pointed out, "aren't divorced."

"Yes, but do they really love each other? I mean, how can you really know? My parents aren't divorced either, obviously, but they sure don't love each other."

"Well, mine do," said Gillian. "And Suzanne and I do."

"Do your parents fight? Do you and Suzanne?"

"Sure, sometimes. Everyone fights."

"If you really love someone," said Lark, "why would you fight?"

Gillian thought a moment, watching Jackie, who was now throwing stones into the water. "Aren't you ever mad at Jackie?"

"Yes."

"Well?"

"Well, what? See? That shows I don't really love him."

Gillian wanted to seize Lark by the shoulders and shake her. How do you prove to someone that anger doesn't necessarily mean lack of love?

But she knew she couldn't shake her.

"Lark, I don't know how to convince you," she said. "I just know it's true. You can be angry at someone and still love them. What you're angry at is what the person *does*, not who they are."

"My parents," said Lark, getting up, "are angry at me because of who I am. Come on. Let's go back. Let's go back and swim or something."

It took Gillian a few minutes to adjust to Lark's change of mood, and when Lark started singing as they rowed back, silly nursery-rhyme songs with Jackie, she found it hard to join in, or even listen. But finally she did, and by the time they got close to the hut again, Gillian realized their laughter was dangerously loud. "Shh," she said as gently as possible. "We'd better quiet down."

"Last one in swimming," whispered Lark as Gillian beached *Sprite* and Lady barked in the distance from inside the hut, "is a rotten egg—and then we'll have lunch, okay? The sun's really high now. We've got carrots today." She hugged Jackie, and climbed out of the boat, saying, "Bunny food for my bunny boy."

She lifted Jackie into the water and, holding his hand, ducked down so that only her head showed. "Gillian," she said, "is a rotten egg! Poor old Gillian."

Ten

GILLIAN WENT HOME to change, after eating carrots and apples with Lark and Jackie, and promising to bring back some milk. Jackie and Gillian between them convinced Lark that he and Lark should keep Lady if no one claimed her; Gillian felt better, knowing they'd have some protection.

I should bring cookies, too, Gillian thought as she neared the end of the path between the hut and the cabin, and bread, and maybe some cheese . . .

"There she is!"

Gillian emerged from her thoughts with difficulty, surprised to see her mother at the door, wearing her painting smock, and Brad on the steps. Neither looked terribly friendly.

"Hi," Gillian called. "What's up?"

Her mother and Brad exchanged a glance. "You're usually home for lunch, Gillian," her mother said with mild reproach. "Brad came over on his break to see you. Margie said she told you before she left for the theater."

"Oh, good grief! She did say something, yes. But I didn't . . ."

"There's sandwich stuff in the fridge," said Mrs. Harrison. "I'm on my way to the field again." She picked up her paint case and easel, and patted Brad's shoulder as she went by.

"I don't have much longer, Gill," said Brad. He regarded her anxiously. "Dad's expecting me back, and I've got to do some cultivating this afternoon while my sister minds the stand. I just wanted to touch base with you after last night. Are you okay?"

"Sure," she said lightly. "Are you?"

"That's not the point." He held the door for her and gestured her in. "Why don't you go change and I'll make you a sandwich?"

"I thought you didn't have much time. Besides, I've had lunch."

Brad was silent a minute. "Your mom said you were swimming with some kids you met."

"Right." Gillian turned away, now alarmed at the—she'd thought—harmless explanation she'd given. Brad knew just about everyone in Pookatasset. She'd have to be more careful if she didn't want to give Lark and Jackie away.

"Who are they?"

"I don't see why you have to give me the third degree!" She made her voice sound exasperated in order to stall for time.

"Gillian, what is wrong with you? If there's some kind of problem, why won't you let me help? Are you and Suze all right? You can tell me; I'm really okay about that. Is . . ."

"Why can't you mind your own business?" she shouted and ran upstairs, slamming the door to her room after her.

And then she sat on the edge of her bed, her face in her hands, sorry she'd yelled at him, and wondering herself what was wrong with her—for she was more edgy than she felt the situation warranted.

It was a lazy, quiet afternoon, peaceful despite the turmoil Gillian knew was inside Lark. She glanced over to where Lark was reading in a poetry anthology Gillian had brought her. Lark seemed to gravitate to the more difficult poems, which supported Gillian's theory that she was very bright. Something about the way she sat there, chin on one hand, lips slightly parted, occasionally mouthing the words of a verse or whispering them, made Gillian want to comfort her, even though she didn't, at least right now, seem to need comforting.

Jackie had gulped down nearly half the fresh milk and devoured the cookies; Gillian decided her allowance could stand to keep him in both without her having to go into her savings. She'd have to bring milk often, though, since of course the only refrigeration Lark and Jackie had was the lake.

Lark looked up, tossing her hair back; it was neater now that she'd used the comb Gillian had brought her. Maybe I could bring her shampoo, too, Gillian thought.

"I like this poem," Lark said shyly.

"Which?"

Lark read:

In my beginning is my end. Now the light falls
Across the open field, leaving the deep lane
Shuttered with branches, dark in the afternoon . . .

"It goes on, but I like the sound of that: 'dark in the afternoon.' "

"T. S. Eliot," Gillian said, sitting beside her. "*Four Quartets.* The part called 'East Coker,' isn't it? I like it, too."

Lark nodded. It was close to four o'clock now and the sun had cooled slightly, though the air remained still and breathless.

"I like this one, too." Lark thumbed back to the beginning of the T. S. Eliot section, and read from "Burnt Norton":

Time and the bell have buried the day,
The black cloud carries the sun away.
Will the sunflower turn to us, will the clematis
Stray down, bend to us; tendril and spray
Clutch and cling?

"It's the sounds I like; I didn't know poems could sing like that. But I guess I never listened before." Lark handed the book back to Gillian.

"Keep it," Gillian told her. "I'll bring you more."

"Sure?"

Gillian smiled. "Sure."

Lark had left the long-sleeved shirt off altogether when she'd changed out of Gillian's bathing suit, and had put on only the T-shirt and shorts. The bandage was grayer now, and frayed.

"I could bring you some tape and gauze," Gillian

95

said hesitantly, nodding toward Lark's wrist. "It's not good to keep a bandage on once it's gotten water on it."

Lark laughed softly. "You take such care of me. Like a mother. We only just met and you take such care of me."

"Looks like someone's got to, doesn't it? You're not taking much care of yourself. Why don't I go get the gauze now? You shouldn't keep that thing on, probably, now that it has gotten wet."

"Don't go."

Gillian had already stood up. "But, Lark . . ."

Lark took Gillian's hand shyly and pulled her down again. "Let's read more poems. The bandage can wait. It doesn't hurt, anyway, at least not much."

"Not much. Then it must hurt some."

"It was pretty deep," Lark said nonchalantly. "Read me a poem. Then I'll read you one."

The sun began its slow descent and Jackie and Lady played a few yards away at the edge of the lake while Lark and Gillian took turns reading poems to each other. Gillian realized that Lark was choosing poems in order to communicate her feelings, so she did the same. But the poems she chose were full of hope, and those Lark chose were increasingly dismal.

By the time they got to the end of the book, Jackie was curled up, his head on Lady's flank, and the sun was close to the tops of the trees across the lake.

"I guess I'd better go," Gillian said. "No, keep it," she insisted when Lark thrust the book at her. "I'll be back, after all. I'll bring you more poems tomorrow. Milk, too," she added, "for Jackie. But you should drink some yourself. And I'll bring that gauze." She stood facing Lark, only a few feet away. "Will you be all right?"

"Sure," said Lark lightly. "Why not? We've been here a week, maybe more. Sure, we'll be all right."

"I'll see you tomorrow then."

But Lark seemed reluctant for her to leave. "What a lot of things are in poems," she said awkwardly. "Layers and layers of them. You think you've seen everything, and then you see another layer underneath."

"My dad says people are like that," Gillian told her. "Layers of meaning, like onions, he says. Lark—I should go."

Lark smiled wistfully. "Okay. See you tomorrow. Onion."

When Gillian had gone partway down the swamp path, she heard Lark call; she turned and Lark was standing there, her hand on Jackie's shoulder. "Hey, Onion," Lark shouted. "Know what? I think I like you!"

Gillian waved. "I like you, too," she answered, feeling warm inside, and hopeful. "Onion."

Her mood shattered as soon as she walked in the kitchen door.

"Where have you been?" her mother asked with uncharacteristic anger, coming into the room.

"Sorry." Gillian went to the sink for a glass of water to cover the guilty feeling that suddenly possessed her. "I guess I am a little late, huh?"

"A little!" her mother exploded. "Do you realize it's quarter past seven? Margie and Peter finally went to the restaurant and I stretched your father's and my dinner to include Brad, who's sitting in the living room trying not to be as mad as I am."

Gillian slammed the glass down on the counter. "Mom, I'm sorry," she said. "I forgot all about it."

"You forgot so much about it," said her mother, "that you didn't even say anything to Brad about dinner when you saw him at lunch. I stopped by the farm stand to get lettuce, and he just happened to be there between trips in from the field, and when I said 'See you tonight,' he was mystified. Gillian, what's going on? Who are those people you were with today, anyway?"

"Just some kids I met down by the lake."

"Boys?"

"Mom!"

"Gillian, if . . ."

Out of the corner of her eye, Gillian saw her father come in from the living room, and saw her mother wave him away. When he was gone, her mother shut the door and sat down at the kitchen table. "Gillian, you're not being yourself," she said more calmly. "It isn't like you to have secrets. It's not fair to us and it's not fair to Brad."

"Mom, don't worry. I'm not seeing another boy, if that's what you're worried about. Look, I'd better go apologize to Brad, huh?"

"Yes, you'd better." Her mother stood up. "Gillian, he cares about you a lot. You haven't been very nice to him since we've gotten here."

Gillian leaned against the sink, her hands wanting to make fists.

"Is there a problem with you two?"

"I don't think so."

"Can't you . . ."

"Mom!" she exclaimed, trying to make it sound like a warning—but her mother caught her arm as she tried to brush by.

"There's such a thing," said Mrs. Harrison softly, "as being too independent."

Eleven

BRAD WAS STIFF and distant while Gillian ate the hamburger her mother hastily broiled for her, and the salad and vegetables. Her parents left them alone—but, Gillian mused, heading for the hut the next morning with a canvas bag of first-aid supplies, they might as well not have, for all the talking she and Brad had done.

The clearing around the hut was silent and empty, and Gillian's heart lurched painfully when she saw a thick oblong of white paper fastened to the hut's door.

Relief swept over her, though, as soon as she read the first line:

Dear Gillian,

Don't panic. This isn't a suicide note. I just wanted to go on talking with you, that's all, and since you weren't here, I decided to write instead. If I get nervous about watching you read this, I'll

100

put it on the door and take Jackie and Lady for a walk. Lady's paw seems a lot better.

I guess I sort of kidnapped Jackie. I didn't tell anyone I was taking him, or ask anyone's permission. He didn't mind coming; he was so scared, Gillian!

It was after I came home from the hospital from trying to kill myself. In the hospital they said I should have counseling and I did talk to a shrink a couple of times but my father said he wasn't going to pay for any such nonsense, and that he'd make me snap out of it himself. He was upset anyway that I'd tried to kill myself because he said it would make him look bad at work if anyone found out. A social worker from the hospital came over the day after I got out—a different one from that time I told you about—but my father wouldn't let her in. He said she was just a busybody.

Anyway, a couple of nights after that, we had another big fight. My father was drunk, worse than I'd ever seen him. He'd just lost his job, like he'd been scared of doing, and he was trying to say it was my fault, that someone must have found out about me and told the boss. Only I didn't see how that could have happened. I still don't. He kept telling my mother she shouldn't have had me, or even Jackie, as if she'd done it all by herself. He said I was a bad person who should never have been born and he slapped me and then he grabbed me and started sort of pushing at me and saying I was ungrateful for everything he'd done for me and all the money he'd spent on me, and he was going to make me stop defying him like the way I did by bringing social workers into the house. I tried to say I didn't have anything to do with that, but he said I must have asked that she come and that I must have said bad things to the shrink about him, and he took his belt off and started waving it around. My mother screamed but she didn't do anything, and then Jackie yelled, "Don't you hurt Larkie!" and he tried to get between me and my father when my father grabbed at me. So then my father grabbed Jackie instead and hit him with the belt. He'd never hit Jackie before, except for slaps, but this was awful; he was really beating him. I couldn't get Jackie away at first, and my mother was just over in the corner, crying. Then my father tripped and I did get Jackie away and took him upstairs.

The next day I told my mother I'd watch Jackie after school while she went shopping, and we split.

It was easier than I thought. I didn't plan it or anything. We just got on a bus and went downtown. We hung around Providence for a while, near the big bus station and near the railroad station. But people kept trying to sell us drugs, and men kept bothering me and we couldn't find any really safe place to sleep. Then I met this girl who was a hooker. She said she was from a town out here where there were summer places she used to break into, so I got us on another bus and we came here.

I'm really sorry I broke into your parents' cabin. It's different when you know the people. Mostly when I steal things I don't think about the people who own them, except that they have more stuff than Jackie and I do. That's how I get myself to do it. That and Jackie. I've got to take care of him till I get him to my aunt's. Sometimes I think I could

leave him at an orphanage or something but I think
they sometimes treat kids badly and my aunt (she's
my mother's sister) is a nice lady. She likes kids
and she loves Jackie and I know she thinks my
mother's in a bad marriage and everything. Maybe
she could even help my mother if she knew more
about what my father's like. I don't know, and I'm
not sure she'll take Jackie but I think she will. And
if she does, then I can decide about me. What I'm
going to do.

Mostly I think I know, though.

Thank you for reading all this.

Now I have to decide whether to tear it up or not.

Lark

Gillian rested her head against the door when she'd
read the note. "God," she whispered. "Oh, please,
God . . ."

Then she sensed someone behind her, and there was
Lark watching her silently. Jackie was behind her,
with Lady.

"Lark . . ." Gillian began.

Lark held up her hand. "Don't say it. Sounds like
a lot of hype, doesn't it? I probably read it all in a
book, or most of it, and made up the rest. Rich imagination, that's what my teachers used to say. I'm supposed to be brilliant, you know. Gifted. High IQ."

Gillian took the four or five steps necessary to reach
her, and folded her in her arms. "Shut up," she said
fiercely, stroking Lark's hair. "Shut up."

Lark's body was rigid at first, but in a while she
relaxed. Then Gillian felt Lark's shoulders shake and
realized she was crying.

"Go ahead," she said, her own eyes filling. "Go

ahead. It's okay, Lark. It's okay. I don't mean the things you said in your letter are okay, because I know they're not. I mean it's okay to cry."

Gillian felt a poke in her side and looked down to see Jackie, trembling a little, obviously frightened. "Don't worry, Jackie." She reached down and put an arm around him, too, as much of him as she could get to. "Lark's just feeling sad today. Don't you feel sad some days?"

Jackie nodded.

"So do I," Gillian said, as much to Lark as to Jackie. "So does everyone. Lark needs to cry for a while. Sometimes that makes people feel better. Okay?"

"Lark hurt herself?" Jackie asked fearfully, his eyes darting to Lark's wrist. "Lark cut herself again?"

"No, honey," Gillian told him. "No, she's sad inside, but she didn't hurt herself on the outside again." She forced a smile. "Hey, Lady's lonely. Look—she wants you to play." Lady was standing anxiously nearby, tail slowly waving, head cocked. "Don't you, Lady?" She picked up a stick and tossed it.

Lady obligingly fetched it, and Jackie, with another worried look at Lark, took it from her and led Lady away.

Gillian eased Lark down on the hut's stone stoop, and sat there holding her till she quieted.

"Nobody," said Lark, looking up at last, her face red and swollen, "ever listened. Or cared. Until you."

"That's a lonely feeling."

"I guess you can understand that." Lark sniffed. "Do you mind that I know about you?"

"No, I'm glad." Gillian tried to smile. "I think you can understand about me and Suzanne better than most people. You don't have to be just like someone else to have a pretty good idea of how they feel. And, Lark? I never told anyone this, but sometimes I feel some of the same things you were talking about before. About the world—bombs, wars, people killing each other. Sometimes I wonder, too, if there's any point to anything I might do—being a forester, or even just being a person. I sort of push it all under, I guess, like most people, or tell myself as long as there's a chance I can help make things better, I might as well try. I think if more people faced the bad things, as you've done, and then tried to do something about them, as you did when you took Jackie away from your father—I don't know. Maybe the bad things could be changed, some of them, anyway. You probably can't change your parents. But that doesn't mean you couldn't help change other things, even the bigger ones, when you grow up."

Lark shook her head, and the bottomless despair in her eyes made Gillian want to look away. "I don't think so," Lark said. "But I think that's the difference between you and me. You're an optimist. You think there's some way to make things better. I'm a pessimist; I don't."

"I think the hard part is finding *how* to work things out. You have to be persistent. But if you are, you usually find a way."

Lark traced a pattern in the dirt with her hand. "I wish I could believe that."

"Keep on wishing," said Gillian, hoping it was the right thing to say, "and maybe you will."

Lark was silent.

"Right now you're very much an onion," Gillian said softly, trying to make her talk again. "So many layers of meaning."

"Too many," said Lark, "to understand."

"Not for a friend, Lark."

Lark stood up. "I never really had one before."

"You do now." Gillian stood also. "If you want."

When Lark didn't answer, Gillian rummaged in the canvas bag she'd brought. "I found some gauze. And I've got tape, too, and scissors. Not to mention peroxide. And another poetry book." She put the book on the stoop and held out her hand. "Dr. Gillian here. Next patient, please."

Lark didn't resist when Gillian sat her down on the stoop again and cut off the grimy bandage. The wound underneath was still red and it was stitched together with six or seven separate black threads. There was a small amount of pus around one of them.

"Shouldn't the stitches come out?" Gillian asked.

"I guess. They said a week or ten days."

"Has it been that long? It must have."

"Longer."

"Well?"

"Oh, sure, go to a hospital or a doctor, with my picture all over the place!"

"But, Lark, they can't stay in indefinitely. This one's already looking yucky."

"They're easy to take out. I've had stitches before. You just cut them and pull them out. It's hard with one hand, but"—Lark looked steadily at her—"you could do it, I bet."

Gillian's mouth went dry. "But I . . ."

"Dr. Gillian," Lark said. "You know I can't go to a real doctor."

Gillian had watched the vet take stitches out of Peter's dog's cut the summer before, and her family's doctor had taken some out of her own finger a few years back. Still, it seemed dangerous.

But it seemed dangerous to leave them in, too.

So, hardly breathing, and tongue between her teeth, Gillian poured peroxide on the scissors, which luckily were small and narrow, and then on Lark's wrist. She lifted a stitch by the strings protruding from its knot, snipped, and pulled.

"The really bad part started when I forgot to get something at the store," Lark said without preamble as Gillian worked. "My father started yelling that I was no good and how come my teachers thought I was so smart if I couldn't even remember to buy something. My mother said not to yell and that we didn't really need whatever it was, but he said that wasn't the point; I was no good anyway, and I wouldn't ever be any good. Then Jackie came in and started crying and he said Jackie was no good, too. But I figured he just said that because he was mad at me. And I thought maybe if I wasn't around he'd notice Jackie more, and maybe like him more, and maybe he'd realize what he'd done to me and wouldn't do the same thing to Jackie. That was before he hit Jackie with the belt."

Gillian tried to keep her hand steady, but she slipped a little, listening as well as working, and Lark winced. "Sorry," said Gillian. "That must have hurt."

"Not really. It just pinched. The next day after school," Lark went on, "I bought some razor blades and for a while it was a good feeling knowing I had them. I'd already been checking the ones in the bathroom, but I was worried they might be all gone just when I needed them. It was scary, thinking about doing it. I'm scared of pain. But it was also sort of comforting, knowing there was something I could do that would make everything stop, and that maybe it would help Jackie. So a few days later when my father was at work and my mother and Jackie were grocery shopping, I drank some booze because I was really tense, and then I went into the bathroom and did it." Lark paused, watching Gillian snip the last stitch. "Like I said, it didn't really hurt at first."

Gillian reached for the peroxide, and realized as she picked it up that she was gripping the bottle much more tightly than necessary, as if her renewed anger at Lark's parents had gone into her hands. "How does it feel now?" she asked, thinking: What a dumb thing to say!

But Lark didn't seem to mind. "It feels funny, more than hurts. Tingly, sort of."

"It looks like it's healing pretty well." Gillian poured peroxide on some gauze. "That infected bit doesn't seem to go very deep. But I'd better put some more peroxide on it just in case."

Lark nodded and Gillian squeezed the wet gauze over the wound.

"There. Let's let it dry for a minute before we bandage it again. I don't know if peroxide burns or not, like alcohol, if it's covered. Don't want to add insult to injury. Or injury to injury."

Lark leaned over and kissed Gillian quickly on the cheek, a child's kiss, innocent and grateful. "Thank you," she said.

"You're welcome." Gillian got up, swallowing hard against the teary lump that threatened to overpower her voice, bowed, and said, "Dr. Gillian, at your service, ma'am."

Lark laughed—but the pain that still lurked in her eyes stayed with Gillian all day, through dinner that evening, and beyond.

Twelve

THAT NIGHT GILLIAN got two phone calls, and her parents, one. One of hers was from Suzanne, saying what time her bus was due on Friday—the next day—and the other was from Brad, asking her to see him Friday night. She said no, because Suzanne was coming, but promised they'd both watch the parade with him Saturday.

Her parents' call was from the police.

Gillian was reading when it came and was so absorbed in her book that she didn't hear her mother call her the first time.

"Gillian!" her mother said insistently, standing in the kitchen dooiway with the phone receiver in one hand. "Didn't you hear? I said Officer Dolan wants to talk to you. He's one of the policemen who came about the break-in. The youth officer," she added.

Gillian put her book down reluctantly, trying to

110

ignore the sudden queasiness in her stomach, and went into the kitchen to the phone. Old lantern-jaw, she thought.

"He has some questions," her mother whispered. "He's got an idea who broke in, and I remembered what you—here, you talk to him." She handed Gillian the receiver, and stood aside, anxiously watching.

"Yes?" Gillian said tensely into the phone. "Officer Dolan? Hi. It's Gillian."

"Hi there, Gillian," said the policeman—too heartily, Gillian thought, as if he's trying to pretend that what he's calling about doesn't really matter. "How're you doing?"

"Fine."

"Great. Listen, Gillian, your mom mentioned that you met some kids the other day, kids she doesn't know, and that you spent quite a while with them. I'm trying to follow up some leads on a thing or two, you know, the break-ins and some other stuff, and I thought those kids you met might know something. Could you tell me their names so I can get in touch with them?"

Gillian searched desperately for a plausible answer. It should, she thought, be as close to the truth as possible, so she wouldn't forget it later. "You know, it's funny," she said, stalling, "but they never told me their last names. Or last name; I think they're brother and sister. I'm—I'm not sure I got their first names right either."

"Give it a shot, okay?"

"Well, let's see. The boy's name might have been—um—Larry, I think he said. I'm less sure of the girl. Maybe Susan?"

111

"You tell me."

Gillian felt her mother watching her and realized she was twisting the phone cord. "Yeah, Susan."

"Okay," said Dolan dryly. "And how old would you say these kids were?"

"Around my age, I guess," Gillian answered, more quickly this time, hoping that would steer him away from Lark and Jackie. "Teenagers, anyway. You don't think they did the break-ins, do you? I don't really know, but I think they're summer people, like us."

"You didn't find out where they live?"

"No. I wasn't with them for very long. Most of the time, we were swimming. We didn't talk much, but they were nice. I didn't want to ask a lot of questions." Gillian licked her dry lips and wished her mother, who was sitting at the kitchen table, would go away. Gillian had never been good at lying; in fact, she'd always hated to lie. Margie was the one who'd been good at it. Not honest Gillian.

"Where'd you go swimming?" Dolan asked, a harsher edge to his voice this time.

"The lake."

"Where at the lake?"

"I'm not sure exactly. I was in the boat . . ." She felt herself start to sweat. Had she been in *Sprite* when she first mentioned meeting the kids? Or had she gotten *Sprite* afterward? Did that matter, though? It was Margie she'd seen when she'd come back for the bathing suits, not her mother, so her mother wouldn't know that. Unless Margie told her . . .

"There's a shed on your parents' property, isn't there? A little shack, almost a kids' playhouse?"

Gillian found she was twisting the cord again, and

her mouth felt dry now, as well as her lips. She tried to swallow. "Yes, but . . ."

"Been over there lately? Now that you folks are here, we haven't been checking your place like we do in the winter. No one was using that shack last time we looked, a while before you arrived, but . . ."

Gillian cleared her throat and said quickly, "Oh, sure I've been there. I like to go there by myself, you know, to think and read and stuff. It's sort of my private place."

"You take those kids there?"

"No. I said it's my private place. I don't take anyone there except people I know really well."

"Umm. Well, listen. If you see those kids again, try to get their last names, okay? Or name, if they do turn out to be brother and sister. It'd help if you found out where they live, too. And be careful who you hang around with. You never know, these days."

"Okay," said Gillian. "Thanks."

"Goodbye for now."

"Goodbye."

Mrs. Harrison stood up as soon as Gillian got off the phone. "Gillian," she began. "Gillian, I . . ." But she stopped. As Gillian tried to go past her into the living room, she put her hand on Gillian's arm. "He said someone had seen a girl around here who looked like a runaway they have a bulletin on. Small, sort of stringy hair, skinny."

Gillian forced a laugh. "Well, the girl I saw yesterday—that Susan or whatever her name is—is pretty fat. Really. There's no way anyone would call her small and skinny, although I guess her hair did look stringy." You're getting too good at this, Gillian, she

113

said to herself, angry that she knew she'd probably have to get even better if she was going to continue to hide Lark and Jackie.

"Gillian." Her mother looked closely at her. "This isn't like you."

"What isn't?" She tried to sound angry, but underneath she was glad the focus had shifted to her. "What have I done, anyway?"

"You aren't acting like yourself, and you know it. Being secretive, and late, forgetting a date with Brad, embarrassing your sister . . ."

"Embarrassing! Just how did I embarrass her?"

"Oh, Gillian, you know perfectly well. Here Margie arranged this nice dinner for you and Brad and you just ignored it. She had something special to tell you, too, and you just . . ."

"What special?"

"That's Margie's business. You'd better ask her. But I know she's very hurt. And I know," Mrs. Harrison went on, fixing Gillian with her eyes, "that you're involved in something you're not telling the truth about, and that worries me, Gillian, very much. You've always been so . . ."

"It's a difficult age," Gillian said nastily. "Aren't all teenagers supposed to be secretive? Of course, the first thing parents are supposed to look for is drugs. Then booze, I think, or is it the other way around? And then . . ."

Gillian felt her mother's hands digging into her shoulders; her mother shook her, something she hadn't done since Gillian was around seven. "Gillian, stop it! I don't know what's come over you, but please, stop it!"

"I'm sorry, Mom." She felt deflated—genuinely

sorry, too, for she and her mother rarely quarreled, and had always been close, although not quite as close as she and her father. "I was rude. I'm sorry."

"You can talk to me, you know," her mother said more gently. "Truly, you can talk to me. I'm not going to judge you, darling, at least I'll try not to. But I do worry about you."

Gillian squeezed her mother's hand. "I know, Mom. I really do. Just trust me, okay? I promise I'll talk to you if I need to."

Later that night, as soon as the house was quiet, Gillian got surreptitiously out of bed, dressed, and padded in her bare feet across the balcony, down the stairs, and out, putting on her sneakers only when she was safely on the back steps. She didn't even switch her flashlight on till she was well along the swamp path to the hut.

The hut was quiet, eerily bathed in moonlight, looking deceptively deserted. Gillian went to the door and knocked softly, then called, "Lark? Lark, don't be afraid, it's Gillian. Lark, wake up. I have to talk to you."

There was a soft bark from inside and a moment later the door opened. Lark stood there, wearing just the long shirt this time, rubbing her eyes. "What's the matter?"

"The cops," said Gillian. "They called." She led Lark outside and paraphrased the conversation she'd had with Dolan.

Lark's eyes didn't change expression, but her shoulders slumped as Gillian talked.

"I'm not sure," Gillian finished, "that Officer Dolan believed me about Susan and Larry. And I bet the cops are going to come out here looking pretty soon. I think they'll need a search warrant to go inside, but I'm not sure, and maybe they'll need Dad's permission to poke around outside. The trouble is, I know he'd give permission, maybe even come over himself. I guess we're lucky no one's searched here so far."

Lark looked smaller; she shivered. "What do I do now?" she asked softly.

"One of two things, I guess. Turn yourselves in—I don't think they'd do much to you, Lark, I really don't, if you told them what you've told me. They might even help." But she thought of the ineffective social worker Lark had mentioned, and she could feel Lark resisting anyway. "Or go someplace else to hide," she added.

"Where?" A wistful smile crossed Lark's face. "I'm not very good at this, running away, I mean, living any old place. Finding your hut was just lucky. I don't know how to live on the street, get food, stuff like that; I'm not good at it, especially in the city. And there's Jackie . . ." She straightened her shoulders. "But I guess I'd better learn, huh? There ought to be some empty summer cabins around here, or old barns or something. Then maybe I could figure out how to get Jackie to New Hampshire. You know, to our aunt's. I guess I'd really better try doing that."

"Don't you think the cops will look in empty cabins and old barns?" Gillian hesitated, then said what she'd been thinking ever since the phone call. "There's an inlet off the lake, with a peninsula, pretty well hidden. There's no road all the way out there; the peninsula's almost an island. You'd be trapped if anyone came, but you'd probably see them before they saw you and you'd probably be able to hide. There's

lots of thick bushes. And"—she took a deep breath—
"we've got some old camping gear stashed away that
no one's used for years. It doesn't look to me as if
anyone's going to use it for years more, either. I could
probably bring you food and stuff, at least for a while."

"That's a risk for you," Lark said vehemently. "It
wouldn't be fair. You shouldn't have to get into trouble, too. I'll feel like poison if you do; you've already
helped so much."

"And I'll feel like poison if you get caught when
you're still—well, still sorting things out." She
paused, then said, "I do think you should turn yourself
in sometime soon, or go to someone who'll be able to
help you, maybe your aunt in New Hampshire, like
you said. But I can't force you to do that, and I guess
you're not ready. I know what it's like to need to think
things over alone."

Lark looked at Gillian for a moment, her eyes bright
with unshed tears, and then pushed past her abruptly,
going farther out into the clearing, in the moonlight.

Gillian let her go, and stood watching her. When
Lark didn't move, though, Gillian went tentatively up
to her.

Lark spoke before Gillian could; her voice was
shaky, but in control. "Okay. Tell me what to do."

"Good." Gillian tried to sound more certain than
she felt. "The first thing is to get you and Jackie to
the inlet."

About ninety minutes later, after they'd made the hut
look deserted again and had loaded *Sprite* so heavily
her gunwales dipped and dragged in the water, Gillian rowed, oars muffled, along the eastern shore of
the lake to the almost invisible inlet, and turned in.

Lark and Jackie were huddled in the bow, Jackie bleary with sleep, and Lark tensely rigid. Lady lay obediently at Lark's feet on the towels and blankets from the hut. The bandage on her paw, Gillian noticed abstractedly, was getting tattered, and very dirty. But it still looked firmly in place.

"Moving day." Lark giggled nervously as Gillian beached the boat on rough pebbles.

"One more trip should do it," Gillian whispered, helping Jackie out. "Let's unload and then I'll go back for the camping stuff."

"I'll come, too." Lark bent over a hastily thrown-together bag of groceries—the pasta, Lady's special food.

"No. It'll be safer if it's just me. I feel I can breathe again now that you're here and the hut's cleared out. No point in taking a chance on your going to my folks' cabin, for lord's sake!"

"What about the chance you'll take? You never think of that!"

"The police aren't looking for me." Gillian tied *Sprite*'s bow line to a branch and shouldered her way through the bushes on the shore, carrying the towels and blankets. "Come on. I think there's a sort of open space up here." I hope, she added silently; it had been two years since she'd explored the inlet and its promontory. Woods could get mighty grown over in two years.

But it seemed just about the same: thick blueberry bushes, giving way to laurel and ground hemlock; then an overgrown field with daisies, Queen Anne's lace, and yellow hawkweed brightening the tall grass—rough, but flat enough to pitch a tent in. She'd

118

have to haul drinking water for Lark and Jackie, though; there was a spring near the hut, but there was none here, and it wouldn't be safe for them to drink lake water. Of course they could always boil it, but she wasn't sure she could trust them to remember.

Beyond the field were beeches, tall and wide and stately, with saplings clustered at their feet like adoring students. Beyond them, Gillian knew, was a tangle of mixed growth and the wide swamp that had kept anyone from building a road. A rough track did come partway, a dirt spur off the main road, but it led only to an abandoned dumping site and was rarely used. It might be handy even so, although if she drove to the peninsula, she'd have to be careful to turn down it only when no one else was passing by.

"I like it." Lark hugged Jackie. "What do you think, punkin? Isn't this a nice place to live?"

Jackie looked dubious, and pale in the moonlight. "No house," he said, pouting.

Lark knelt in front of him. "No, but Gillie's going to bring us a tent. Won't that be fun?"

"Like Indians, Jackie." Gillian knelt, too, seeing he was close to tears. "You'll be camping out, living the way the Indians did."

"Want to be a pirate," Jackie whined.

Gillian supressed a chuckle. "Well, what do you think pirates do when they're shipwrecked? Camp out, that's what!"

"And hide," said Lark, "very cleverly and quietly, so no one will find them."

Jackie's face cleared momentarily, but then crumpled and collapsed into tears. "Want to go home," he wept, clinging to Lark.

Lark held him close and rocked him, her eyes stricken. "Oh, punkin, punkin, we can't go home. We can't. We've got to stay here."

"Forever?"

"No, not forever. I'm probably going to take you to Aunty's, remember?"

"Want to go to Aunty's now."

Lark looked up; Gillian held Lark's eyes with her own. "You can't go now, Jackie," Gillian said. "It's nighttime now. And it's a long way. Look." She stood up. "I'm going to make you and Lady a nice bed right here on this soft grass, and then I'm going back to get a tent and some sleeping bags and things. If you're a very good boy and go to sleep now, you can help us put the tent up. Hey, Mate Peg-leg." She touched his tear-dampened face with the tip of her finger. "I've got to leave you in charge of the prisoner." She pushed Lark gently; Lark obligingly fell forward and moaned, "Mercy, mercy!" Then her eyes darted craftily around the clearing and she said under her breath, "I bet I could escape over there under those trees. I bet there's a way out there, and I could swim to my ship."

"No." Jackie seized her arm. "You'll have to walk the plank. We'll make you."

"No, no, not the plank!" cried Lark, giving Gillian a quick, grateful glance. "Not the plank."

"Here." Gillian rummaged under the pile of blankets and towels, took out the larger towel and rolled it into a long strip. "Tie 'er up, Matey. I'll be back in a jiff with supplies. Yo-ho-ho!"

"Yo-ho-ho," answered Jackie, struggling with the towel, his eyes dry, but his face still streaked with tears.

Thirteen

GILLIAN HAD ESTABLISHED when she'd gone back for *Sprite* that the camping gear was stored under the house, and before she'd left, she'd collected some paper and pencils and two books from the case in her room, making as little noise as possible—*Winnie-the-Pooh* for Lark to read to Jackie and a Shakespeare anthology for Lark. The Shakespeare seemed hard for a fourteen-year-old, but since Lark had liked T. S. Eliot, Gillian reasoned she might like this as well. Besides, she thought as she loaded *Sprite* and stowed the books and paper carefully in a fold of the tent, we started reading Shakespeare in school when we were Lark's age.

By dawn, they had a fair camp, with the Harrisons' old tent firmly staked and two sleeping bags stashed neatly inside. Gillian made a lean-to with branches and tarp, under which she put the towels, Lady's food, two full water bottles, and a cooler. "Any food that's open or loose," she instructed Lark, "keep in the cooler, even if it doesn't have to stay cool. Otherwise, you'll have lots of four-legged visitors. Here." She handed Lark the books. "Give you something to do. Jackie might like *Pooh* read to him. And there's a pad of paper on the cooler, and a couple of pencils. I'll see if I can find a coloring book for him when I'm in the village, and some crayons. But I don't think I'll be able to come back for a couple of days. Suzanne's coming for a visit; I think I told you."

Lark looked up from the books. "Good," she said softly, touching Gillian's arm. "You'll be happy."

"Yes. I miss her, very much. Anyway, you're safe here, I'm sure. And"—she pointed to the lake, whose shimmer was just visible through the blueberry bushes—"look, the sun's coming up."

"Don't tell me it's a new beginning," Lark said bitterly. "Or that I'll feel better. Don't tell me that."

"I won't," said Gillian, hurt. It was a struggle sometimes, talking to Lark; it would be a relief to lose her temper. But she patted Lark's shoulder instead. "I'd better get back before I'm missed. And you'd better get some sleep. Okay? You'll . . ." She stopped herself; she had been going to say Lark would feel better, after all.

Lark didn't seem to notice. "I'll try to sleep," she said. "Thank you for the books and stuff."

"You're welcome." Gillian started walking away, then turned back. "Write it down," she called, "if things get bad. You know. Like that letter you wrote before. Would you?"

"I might."

Gillian stood a moment longer, watching her. Jackie had gone into the tent with Lady, and Lark was standing next to it, dwarfed by both it and the surrounding space. She looked tiny, vulnerable.

"Suze leaves Monday morning," Gillian called. "I'll try to get away before then, but I promise I'll come Monday."

"What's today?" asked Lark.

"Thursday—no, Friday, now. Look, if I can, I'll bring you some food this weekend. I'll just put it on the shore if I can't stay, so keep checking there, under bushes. But try to make what you have last till Monday. I don't think you should risk stealing more. No —I know you shouldn't. Please don't."

"I wish I could get out," Lark said. "I wish you didn't have to wait on me. I wish I could pay you or do something for you. I wish . . ."

Gillian went back to her, gripped her shoulders. "Remember how good it makes me feel that you understand about Suzanne and me. About just me, too. So you've already done something."

"It's not enough."

"Yes, it's enough. A friend is special. You're a friend."

"Not enough of one."

Gillian had no reply to that, except, "I think you are."

And then she left.

It was all she could do to keep her eyes open at breakfast and to drag herself through the day, trying to stay outwardly cheerful and nonchalant. She did manage to call Dr. Morelli and establish that no one had claimed Lady so far, and she also finally managed to trim some of the bushes where the Harrisons' driveway met the main road; her father was pleased.

Finally at around three-thirty, Gillian and her parents drove into Providence to pick Suzanne up at the bus.

Suzanne wouldn't betray Lark and Jackie, she kept saying to herself on the way; not like Brad. He might turn them in, thinking he was doing the right thing, but Suzanne wouldn't, not if I explained.

It's no good, Gillian, she answered herself back tiredly. The fewer people you involve, the better. And you know it wouldn't be fair to Suzanne; it would put her in a terrible position, especially if it *is* illegal to help runaways.

The neighborhood around the bus station was sleazy, and before Suzanne's bus came in, Gillian saw two girls in short skirts and stiletto heels lurking around the newsstand. Would Lark have to be like them, she wondered, if she came back to the city? The girls didn't seem much older than Lark, certainly no older than Gillian. She wondered if one of them could be the hooker who'd told Lark about Pookatasset.

When the New York bus arrived, Suzanne literally jumped off, frowsy blond hair bouncing around her face, and yards of beads, as usual, draped around her neck. She waved and shrieked, and mouthed jokes to Gillian and her parents as she waited with the other passengers for her bags to be unloaded from the bus's luggage bay.

Gillian felt herself smiling. Oh, it was good to see her!

"That girl never changes," said Mrs. Harrison affectionately. "I bet she'll have the same frantic energy at forty-five as she does now."

"Shouldn't wonder," said Professor Harrison. He was smiling, too.

"There's her bag, Alex."

"Right." Gillian's father strode through the crowd to the bus's side and picked up an obviously heavy blue suitcase. It was a family joke, and had been for years, that Suzanne needed a trunk to go on an overnight. "It's lucky she never went camping," Mrs. Harrison had commented often enough—but then she had gone, with them, and never touched the mountain of clothes she'd brought with her.

Her luggage secured, Suzanne ran to Gillian and her mother and enveloped them both in an enormous hug, kissing Gillian's cheek and giving her hand a private squeeze. "Oh, Harrisons, it's good to be here!" she said, beaming. "New York's a stinking sewer. I can't wait to get in the lake. Gillian, you'd just die, you know old Mrs. Claremont, in your building? Well, I was going past there last night, and she was out in the street, walking her dog . . ."

"Horrors," said Professor Harrison, shepherding them to the car. "And in broad daylight, too!"

Suzanne giggled. "Yes, but she was in her nightgown. No coat or anything, even, over it."

"Poor soul," said Mrs. Harrison. "I was afraid something like that would happen."

"I know; she'd be a positive bag lady if they'd let her. But you know how the doormen take care of her, and they did this time, too. I put my sweater on her, and led her back, and one of the doormen took her and the dog upstairs. But you'd have died. I mean, I nearly split laughing afterward, even though it's kind of sad. Gillian," she went on, grabbing Gillian's arm, "I got your letter . . ."

By now they were in the car, Gillian and Suzanne in the back, and Professor and Mrs. Harrison in the front. The professor piloted the car carefully through the busy streets—it was the beginning of the evening rush hour—and Gillian, her eyes burning from lack of sleep, stared out moodily, wishing she and Suzanne were alone, and thinking again of Lark. Could a person be a bag girl before becoming a bag lady? She did want to tell Suzanne; she ached to.

"So," said Suzanne, "you said Brad's fine?"

"Yes."

Mrs. Harrison turned around. "Brad *seems* fine, Suze, but Gillian hasn't seen as much of him as he'd like, I think. She's made some new friends, too."

"Yeah? Anyone special?"

Gillian panicked, momentarily blanking on the names she'd made up. "Well, one's a girl," she said lamely. Then she remembered. "Susan, her name is. And she's got a brother—um—Larry." She made a mental note to remember that she'd now said definitely they were brother and sister and that the girl's name really was Susan.

"I think this Larry must be pretty cute," said Mrs. Harrison, still facing toward the back. Her neck'll crack, Gillian thought irritably; why doesn't she turn around?

Suzanne gave Gillian a shrewd look. "Oh, yeah?" she said dryly. "How about that?"

Gillian smiled noncommittally. They were out of the city now, on the open highway, passing a field of grazing cows. "Look," she said to change the subject, pointing. "A calf—there, see? A tiny one."

"Ever the countrywoman," said Suzanne. "How's the farm doing?"

It took Gillian a moment to realize Suzanne meant

126

Brad's farm, and then she realized she hadn't even visited there yet this summer. "Okay, I guess."

"See what I mean, Suze?" said Mrs. Harrison. "I think this Larry must really be something."

Mrs. Harrison turned back at last. As soon as she did, Suzanne reached for Gillian's hand and held it tightly until they got to the cabin.

Later, when they were alone in Gillian's room, changing for a swim, and Suzanne had thrown her suitcase on the cot they'd set up for her, and they'd kissed properly and held each other for as long as they dared, Suzanne looked shrewdly at Gillian and said, "Okay, Gill, what's up? You look awful. Come on, tell me."

Gillian shook her head, despite the ache inside.

"Uh-uh. You don't get away with that stuff with me. What is it? Brad's being a pest? He doesn't believe it about us, after all? He's being rotten? Hurt?" She broke off, studying Gillian's face. "That's not it, right?"

"Right."

"So what is?" Suzanne snapped open her suitcase and began tossing clothes on the cot, finally pulling out a black-and-white-striped bikini. "Like it?" she said, holding up its top. "Sexy, huh?"

Gillian nodded, and fumbled with her own bathing suit while Suzanne changed.

"Ta-dah!" Suzanne whirled, arms out, displaying her suit. "I bought it just for you."

Gillian smiled. "I bought mine for you, too. Yours looks great." She put her arms around Suze again, giving herself the luxury of noticing how smooth her skin was, how comfortably Suze's body fit against her own.

"You look pretty good yourself," Suzanne whispered. She pushed Gillian away gently. "That red suit's terrific. But you look like you haven't slept for about a year, and there must be a reason for that. Is it that sort of adventure you couldn't tell me about? Come on, Gillie."

"I'm fine, Suze, really. Hey, let's go, okay? You're the one who was dying for a swim."

Suzanne stopped her. "You're lying that you're fine. I don't want that swim till I know what's wrong."

"Maybe I can't tell you, Suze."

"What do you mean you can't tell me?"

"Just what I said. It involves other people. I want to tell you, but I have to figure it out first, okay? Trust me, please? It isn't us, it isn't . . ."

"Of course I trust you," said Suze, giving her a long, searching look. "But whatever it is, it looks like it's making mincemeat of you inside, and that scares me. Promise you'll tell me later?"

"Of course. As soon as I can."

Fourteen

IT WAS A STILL MORNING, breathless and heavy, with a steamy haze lying over the lake when Gillian got up, leaving Suzanne gently snoring on her cot. She went down to the beach and stood next to where she'd beached *Sprite*, watching the morning.

Worrying about Lark, too, and Jackie, their first night in the tent.

But it hadn't rained, and the chance of anyone's going out to the point seemed almost nil. Even if someone did, Lark would have the sense to use their story about camping out; who could dispute it with evidence all around?

Unless, of course, it was the cops who found them, or someone who'd seen their pictures in the supermarket.

They would run out of milk soon, at the rate Jackie guzzled it down.

"*There* you are!"

It was Suzanne, fresh in red shorts and a red-and-white shirt, her face wide awake and shining. Suze was one of those people who wake up as if they'd never slept, not like Gillian, who needed gallons of cold water before her eyes opened properly, let alone focused. She'd used lake water this morning; it was still early enough in the summer for it to be cool.

"You sure went out like a light last night," said Suzanne. "Just as well, probably. Hey—let's go for a before-breakfast row."

Silently, Gillian loosened the bow line and pushed *Sprite* off. "I didn't get much sleep the night before," she told Suzanne when they were both aboard. "You sleep okay?"

"Like a baby. What time's that parade?"

"Ten. We're meeting Brad there, okay?"

"Sure. It'll be nice to see him again." Suzanne dipped her hand in the water and waggled it lazily. "Gill, is Margie going to marry Peter like I imagined in my letter?"

"Margie?" Gillian realized the question had startled her. But it made sense, too. "Yes," she said. "I guess she might. Why?"

"Something in her eyes when she looks at him. Kind of like the way you look at me sometimes."

"Yeah?"

"Yeah." Suzanne bent forward, kissing Gillian, then lost her balance and tipped the boat dangerously close to capsizing.

"Some sailor you are," Gillian said when they and the boat were steady again and she'd finished laughing.

"But a refreshingly impulsive lover, you have to admit."

130

They went to the center of the lake, and waved to early-morning fishermen, and Gillian, again fighting the urge to tell Suze about Lark and Jackie, deliberately kept her back to the inlet until she couldn't stand it any longer. Finally she turned and looked. She was relieved and then alarmed to see a curl of smoke hanging lazily above it.

Anyone could see that smoke; she'd have to get word to Lark.

"Wow, am I hungry!" said Suze. "It just hit me, you know, the way it does sometimes. Hit hard." She clutched her stomach and rolled her eyes, but Gillian, though she managed a smile, couldn't quite laugh.

"Better get you home, then." Gillian spun *Sprite* around and rowed back with long, steady pulls of her oars.

Breakfast was enormous, and Margie and Peter, who were moving down to the theater after the parade, were full of last night's dress rehearsal for the first show of the season, which was to open that night. Margie had a small but demanding part, and Peter, as usual, was stage manager.

"I almost screwed up the only big light cue in the whole show," Peter announced between mouthfuls of egg and bacon.

"Almost is almost," Margie remarked fondly.

Gillian studied her; Suze was right about the way Margie looked at him. Then she remembered that Margie had been going to tell her something—Brad, too, presumably—the night she hadn't shown up for dinner, so she cornered Margie in the kitchen after breakfast and asked her what it was.

"Oh, so now you're interested?" Margie chided her,

waving her dishtowel airily. "You couldn't have cared less the other night."

"Come on, Margie, I'm sorry. I've got things on my mind."

"Trees, I bet. It sure can't be Brad. Or maybe it's those kids you said you met?"

"Maybe. Look, I'm sorry, okay? I do want to know, really. If you still want to tell me."

Margie smiled then, as if she couldn't help herself, and said, "Well—how would you like Peter for a brother-in-law?"

Gillian felt herself grin. "Good old Suze; she guessed it! I can't think of anyone I'd rather have for a brother-in-law," she said truthfully, and then hugged her sister. "Oh, Margie, I'm so glad!"

"Me, too, hon." Margie returned Gillian's hug. "And the thing I hope for you more than anything in the world," she said softly, "is that you'll love someone someday the way I love Peter. I'd hoped it might be Brad . . ."

Gillian turned away. "Sorry," she said, shouting inside, *I do love someone; I know how you feel.*

"I know it's not going to be Brad," Margie was saying. "But there'll be someone someday, Gillie, and it's the most wonderful exciting tingly thing in the whole world, just you wait!"

Gillian ran water in the sink for the dishes and squirted detergent into the dishpan.

"Did I say something?"

"No, it's okay."

"I know a girl can be pretty lonesome at seventeen," Margie said quietly. "I think the summer I was seventeen was the worst in my whole life. But you'll see.

You'll be out there in Oregon soon, with all those great-looking guys . . ."

"Someone say something about great-looking guys?" asked Suzanne, winking at Gillian as she bounced into the kitchen and took Margie's dish towel away from her. "Here, let me earn my keep." She looked from Margie to Gillian and back again. "Or am I interrupting something?"

"Nope," said Gillian, glad that Suze was there. "No. Margie just confirmed your suspicions. She and Peter are engaged. Or was that a secret?" she asked anxiously, turning back to her sister. "You were going to tell Brad, too, weren't you? And Suze is . . ."

Margie laughed. "I guess it's not a secret anymore. It's just that we're not going to make it official until fall, when we get the ring and set the date and stuff. Yes, we were going to tell Brad. And, Suze, you're family. Just don't tell *The New York Times*." Margie glanced at her watch. "Whoops, I'd better leave the dishes to you two, okay? I've still got to finish packing before the parade."

Pookatasset's tiny main street was always so jammed with cars and people well in advance of the parade, and parking was always so scarce, that the Harrisons decided to walk to the village. By the time they'd nearly gotten there, they'd paired off, Professor and Mrs. Harrison in the lead, hand in hand, and Margie and Peter next, also hand in hand, followed by Gillian and Suzanne. "It's a trend," said Suzanne, nodding toward the clasped hands. "What the heck? We're engaged, too." She took Gillian's hand, but dropped it almost immediately, saying, "Darn it, there's Brad."

133

Gillian looked to where Suzanne was looking and saw Brad threading his way toward them through the rapidly thickening crowd. "Gillian! Suzanne!" he called, and they both, somewhat reluctantly, waved.

"Hi," he said when he reached them, and for a moment the three of them stood there smiling self-consciously. "It's great to see you again," Brad said, and at almost the same time Suzanne said, "Nice to see you, Brad," and then all three of them laughed. "No hard feelings?" Suzanne asked softly, and Brad, looking embarrassed, shook his head. "Gillie says you've got a new girlfriend," Suzanne went on, and they walked, chatting, another few minutes, until they were in the thick of the crowd, hunting for a good viewing spot with Gillian's parents. They finally found one halfway up a hill that edged the main road, at one end of the town cemetery, among the gravestones.

Brad seemed tense, still, as if he had to make an effort to relax. "This parade's so spectacular," he joked to Suzanne, "that no one misses it, not even the oldest residents. Why, Mr. Burnside here"—he nodded toward the nearest gravestone—"has been coming since"—he bent closer to the stone—"1847."

"Wow!" Suzanne smiled at him, and Gillian could see she was making an effort, too. "I always thought it was a pretty good parade. No one that old's ever at the one on Long Island that my folks go to, although when I was really little I used to think people that old marched in it."

There was a cheer down the road, and a distant sound of sirens and music, and then for the next half hour everyone's attention was riveted on the street, along which passed first the town's prize hook and

134

ladder, complete with coach dog in fireman's hat, and then the police band, followed by assorted floats and marching citizens of all ages. Jackie would love this, Gillian thought as a clown went by, tossing candy to the children; she wished she could have brought him.

At the end of the parade, as the rest of Pookatasset's fire engines rolled by, followed by others, Brad draped one arm almost casually over Gillian's shoulder, and the other one over Suzanne's. Mrs. Harrison, who'd been standing a little distance away with Margie, Peter, and the professor, walked over to them; the others followed. "That's it for this year, I'm afraid. Suze, I keep thinking you must want to see that Long Island one again someday; ours is so pokey."

"I love this one, Mrs. Harrison. It's much more fun. The Long Island one's too grand for me. Heck, it's probably even grander than it was the last time I saw it—what?—seven years ago. No thanks. I'll take Pookatasset's any day."

"I'm glad, dear. We'd miss you if you weren't here. Now, who's doing what today? Margie and Peter are going to the theater, I know . . ."

"And they'd better hurry." Peter bent to kiss her cheek. "We'll see you tonight after the show. Hope you enjoy it."

"We can't wait," said Mrs. Harrison, and the professor asked, "Curtain at eight-thirty, right?"

"Right," Margie answered. "You'll have plenty of time for a great seafood dinner at that place I told you about. I know you'll love it—lobsters, Gillian. And you're invited, Brad, too; we gave Dad an extra ticket."

"Thanks," said Brad.

135

"I know you'll have to miss the fireworks here," said Margie, "but there are some down on the shore. I don't think they start till late, so you might be able to see them after the show."

"Well, that takes care of tonight," said Mrs. Harrison. "But what about the rest of the day? I'm taking the day off, and so's Alex. Anyone for a picnic? Or, Brad, did you have plans with the girls? You don't have to work, I hope!"

"No, not really. A picnic would be fine, Mrs. Harrison. Okay, Gillian, Suze?"

Suzanne nodded, and Gillian, thinking quickly that she might be able to sneak away to the inlet, depending on where they decided to eat, said, "Sure, why not?"

"Let's get hopping then," said the professor briskly. "We'll need sandwich makers and packers, right, Barb? If we all work together, we ought to be able to get everything done before starvation sets in."

There were too many of them to fit easily into *Sprite* along with the picnic things, so Brad went home for his boat, and rowed Suzanne and Gillian, while the professor and Mrs. Harrison followed in *Sprite*. Gillian sensed that both Suzanne and Brad were uncomfortable again; she knew she certainly was, and she tried desperately to find something to say that would ease the tension. But then Brad said it, when they'd passed a sailboat and were bobbing up and down in its wake. "You two look great together, you know? It's right; the more I think about it, it's right. So could we just sort of all go on from there? You keep looking at me, Gillie, like you think I'm mourning or something, but

136

I'm okay. Fine, in fact." He patted his breast pocket. "I got a letter from Michelle yesterday. She's coming home in a couple of weeks." He grinned. "It was a *good* letter."

Suzanne smiled. "I can see why Gillie always liked you, Brad. You're quite a guy, you know?"

"It's great about Michelle, Brad," Gillian said, relieved, and he looked relieved, too.

They'd all agreed on a spot not far from the inlet, at Gillian's urging, and at around 2:30, when everyone was sitting there lazily trying to decide whether to play ball or go for a swim, she stood up, stretched elaborately, and said, "If you folks will excuse me, I've got to go pick some daisies."

Suzanne jumped to her feet. "Good idea. I'll come with you."

"Suzanne," said Gillian, "there are some things a girl has to do alone."

"Don't be a jerk." Suzanne linked her arm cozily in Gillian's. "It's only me. See you in a jiff," she said to Gillian's parents and Brad.

Helplessly, Gillian led Suzanne into the underbrush. "Suze," she said when they were out of earshot of the others, "do me a favor. Do what you have to do and go back without me? Say I've got a stomachache or—I know—say I've lost my pocketknife and am looking for it."

"Gillian?"

"Just trust me. Please? It's really important. And someday, when we're both old ladies sitting in rocking chairs on our porch, I'll tell you all about it."

Suzanne looked uncertain. "Gillian, are you meeting someone? Something to do with that adventure

137

you mentioned in your letter? It's not that I'm jealous or anything, at least I don't think I am—but, hey, can't I play, too?"

"You don't know how much I wish you could, except it's not playing. Really. I'm just not sure yet . . ." She broke off, seeing the doubt on Suzanne's face; she took Suzanne's hands. "Look, Suze, it—what I'm doing might be—well, sort of illegal. I don't know. I just don't want to involve you if it is, okay?"

"Illegal? For Pete's sake, Gillian!"

"It's not drugs; it's not anything like that. I just have to help someone, that's all. I'm a little scared, maybe more than a little. But I have to do it."

"If you're scared, then I want to help, too. I want to even if you're not scared. Why can't I?"

"I told you, I don't want to risk your getting into trouble. And besides, I'm not sure you could help; I'm not sure they'd let you. Suze, I've got to go. Please. Tell everyone I lost my knife. I hate lying, but . . ."

"Just don't lie to yourself, Gillian," Suzanne said, letting her go at last. "Or, in the end, to me."

Fifteen

LARK WAS SITTING in front of the tent in the sun, her hair wet and gleaming, the Shakespeare in her lap, and clean wet clothes, hers and Jackie's, strung along the tent ropes. Jackie was at her feet, scribbling on a piece of paper, and Lady was on her side next to him.

Gillian watched them for a second, till a small bird fluttered in a branch overhead and began to trill lustily.

Lark looked up at it, then met Gillian's eyes and smiled, standing up.

Before Gillian could greet her, Jackie said, "Hi, Gillie. See my picture?" He displayed a dark pencil scrawl.

"That's very good, Mate Peg-leg." Gillian returned Lark's smile. "I can't stay. I just came to tell you that I saw smoke from your fire when I was on the lake this morning. It could give you away. Just use the camp stove, okay?"

"I don't know how."

"Oh, Lark, I'm sorry! Where is it?"

Lark pointed to the lean-to, and Gillian, cursing having to hurry, hastily took it out to a large flat rock in the clearing and showed Lark how to fit the small propane bottle to the stove's pipe. "Matches?"

"Under there."

Gillian rummaged where Lark pointed, found the matches, and demonstrated how to open the valve and hold the lit match against the burner. "Then, when you're through, just turn the burner off," she explained. "Be careful not to leave the valve open without the match there. Dad always says to strike the match first, before you turn on the gas. It's easier with two people, I'm afraid."

"I'll manage." Lark tipped her head toward the tent ropes. "I managed laundry." Then she put her hand on Gillian's arm. "How's Suzanne?"

"Suzanne's okay. It's wonderful to be with her, even if there are other people around all the time. You were smart to do laundry. What did you do for soap?"

"I stole some, back in Providence. Bath soap, but it works." She hesitated. "Did you tell Suzanne about me and Jackie?"

"No."

"Thank you. Gillian?"

"Hmm?"

"I missed you. It was lonely without you. I'm always lonely, but this time I was more lonely than I've been."

"I'm sorry, Lark."

"I guess that comes from having a friend."

"I guess," Gillian replied awkwardly.

"Did you miss me?" Lark asked. Then she moved away. "Of course you didn't, not with all those people. Suzanne and everyone."

Gillian went toward her, and before she knew what was happening, Lark had whirled around and was clinging to her, her face buried against Gillian's shoulder. "Come back soon," Lark whispered. "Come back soon."

"I will. As soon as I can." She hugged Lark gently, and smiled at Jackie, who was watching them, his face very solemn. She felt how thin and fragile Lark's body was, more than her brother's. Like the bird she's named for, Gillian thought.

"Larkie okay?" Jackie asked.

"Yes, punkin, I'm okay." Lark moved away from Gillian quickly and gave him a pat. "I'm fine." She turned back to Gillian, her eyes huge and liquid, still. "I really am."

"Sure?"

"Sure. You have to go."

"I'm afraid so. No fires, okay?"

"I needed a big one for the laundry water. But okay. No more."

Gillian left, but she felt Lark's eyes following her until she was far out of sight.

When Margie spoke her first line, Gillian felt Brad squeeze her hand. She squeezed back nervously, but Margie was fine, and soon Gillian relaxed into pride. Margie's part was unlike her personality: a sullen, despondent younger sister of the heroine; and it struck Gillian, as Margie grumbled her lines and sulked and lost her temper, that she herself might have seemed a little like that recently.

When she mentioned it to Margie, though, later, outside the dressing rooms when Margie was flushed and excited as she always was after a performance, Margie just mussed Gillian's hair affectionately and said, "Hey, Gill, everyone's grumpy now and then. I've never felt as bad as that kid I play, and I hope you haven't either; you certainly never acted that way. But I've felt bad enough to be able to imagine the rest."

It turned out that they'd missed the fireworks, so they all went out for a snack to a small rustic bar and restaurant that was full of other people from the theater. "Wow," Suzanne breathed as Peter led them to a long table in the back, through clusters of chattering theater people, "I can't stand it! All this glitter!"

Peter laughed, and pulled a bench out so Professor and Mrs. Harrison could ease their way in; he and Margie sat next to them. "You wouldn't say that if you saw them at rehearsal at ten o'clock in the morning. Theater people are just like everyone else, only noisier. Now"—he looked at Brad and Gillian, who, with Suzanne, were sitting opposite him and Margie—"I recommend the South County Burger for anyone who's hungry."

"Sounds good," said Brad.

"How anyone can eat after the big lobster dinner we had," Mrs. Harrison began, but the professor put his hand over hers and she stopped.

Gillian passed up the burger and had a large Coke instead. The air outside had grown oppressive, she'd noticed as they'd left the theater, heavy and thick, as if a storm was brewing. She remembered with consternation that the tent was no longer as waterproof as it once had been, and that she'd forgotten to tell Lark that the extra tarpaulin she'd brought with the rest of the camping gear could be rigged as a fly over it, to keep it dry. But maybe it wouldn't rain; maybe the storm would go out to sea . . .

"So you might as well take my station wagon back with you tonight," Peter was saying to the professor.

"That's sweet of you, Peter," said Mrs. Harrison. "But are you really sure? And Margie, how about you? Wouldn't you like the use of Peter's car?"

"I don't need it, Mom. There's not going to be enough time to use it, anyway."

Suzanne poked Gillian under the table; Brad was staring at her. "What?" she asked, confused.

"Boy, you were a million miles away!" Brad looked amused. "Peter just said the theater's given him the use of their van for the summer, for himself as well as to collect props and furniture, so he and Margie won't need the station wagon. They've offered the wagon to you, Gillian. How about that?"

"That—that's great." Gillian wondered for a second if she'd really use it and almost immediately thought of hauling food and water to Lark and Jackie; of course she'd use it. "Great! Thank you."

"You're welcome." Peter leaned back as the waitress came with a tray of food. "You might as well drive it home tonight, since there are so many of you. You might be more comfortable in two cars."

"Very generous," said Professor Harrison. "Only remember to tell us right away if you need it, or even if you just want it. On a day off, for instance."

Peter laughed, and bit hungrily into his South County Burger. "In stock, Professor Harrison, especially for stage managers, days off are usually a myth. Or are just for sleeping. Don't worry about that. Last season, I only had one, if I remember right."

The air was still oppressive when they all left the restaurant. It was decided that Brad, Gillian, and Suzanne would take Peter's station wagon while Professor and Mrs. Harrison drove Peter and Margie back to the inn at which they both had rooms for the season.

Heat lightning flashed on the horizon as Gillian walked with Brad and Suzanne across the parking lot.

"Neat car," said Brad, appraising the station wagon when they reached it. As Gillian unlocked the door with the key Peter had given her, he walked around to the passenger side, then grinned sheepishly and said, "Whoops. I forgot. I guess I should get in the back, right?"

"Right," Gillian said, a little shortly, embarrassed. She slid into the driver's seat, then twisted around to unlock the other doors. "Oh, heck, Brad, sit wherever you like."

Brad held the passenger door for Suzanne and opened the back door at the same time. "The back's fine," he said quietly. "It just takes a while to adjust, you know? We haven't been alone together that much, the three of us." He got into the back seat.

Suzanne glanced at Gillian, then turned around to face Brad. "There's no subtle way to say this, but I'm sorry if it's been hard for you. We really thank you—a lot—for understanding."

"No problem," Brad replied gruffly.

Gillian turned the key and the car responded smoothly. She tried to concentrate on the fact that even though it was larger than the Toyota, it seemed just about as easy to maneuver.

There was an awkward silence as Gillian headed out to the main road.

"Whew, it's hot," Brad said at the same time as Suzanne said, "I wish I could meet Michelle . . ." Brad won, though, talking through her words, saying, "Hope we get home before the storm hits," and Suzanne complied smoothly by asking, "What storm?"

"The one we're going to have tonight. It said on the radio that thunderstorms were likely. Looks like there's a doozy a few miles from here; we'll get it in a while, I bet."

Maybe I can sneak out later, thought Gillian; maybe Suze will sleep soundly again.

There was another silence.

"It really is okay," Brad said. "I thought you knew that from what I said before. I don't know a lot about—you know. But if that's the way you are, that's the way you are. Like I said, you seem good together, happy. And I can see it now, looking back, see that it's—I don't know, logical, I guess, sort of. Besides, Michelle is . . ."

Gillian tried to concentrate on what Brad was saying, and on driving, since there was nothing she could do about the tent till later. Then Brad changed the subject to Margie and Peter, and the possible difficulty of having two people doing the same kind of thing in the same family. "Could be tough," he said. "Except for farming, of course. That's a family business. There's a job for everyone, even the kids. No time for competition, either."

"It's a dying business, though, Brad, isn't it?" Suzanne asked—and in a few minutes Gillian had tuned out again; it was a conversation she'd had with Brad a hundred times before.

Brad, it turned out, had left his jacket in the professor's car, so Gillian turned down the driveway to the cabin instead of going on to the farm to drop him off. The three of them sat around the kitchen table, Suzanne and Brad talking farming and Gillian trying to, until Gillian's parents arrived.

"You'll be wanting this," the professor said, holding out the jacket. "I'm glad you waited for it. The temperature's dropped and the rain's started; going to be quite a storm, I think."

"How about some cocoa?" asked Mrs. Harrison.

"No, thanks," said Brad. "I'd better be going, if it's going to be as bad as you say, Professor Harrison. Thanks for the jacket—sorry I was so dumb!"

"No trouble," said the professor. "I'll run you over in the car, though. There's no sense in your getting soaked even if you do have your jacket back."

"That's okay, Professor Harrison. I bet I can outrun the worst of it—thanks, anyway. Good night, everyone." He smiled at Suzanne and held out his hand. "Nice seeing you again, Suze. Maybe we can all do something tomorrow, once I'm through at the farm. Go to the beach, maybe, if it clears. I mean the real beach, the ocean."

"What a good idea!" Mrs. Harrison patted Brad's shoulder. "Somehow we never get down there, with the lake and all. I could make you a picnic . . ."

"Oh, Mom," said Gillian irritably, "maybe it'll still be raining."

They all looked at her, and she said self-consciously,

"Let's decide tomorrow, that's all I mean. Maybe it won't be a beach day."

"Hopeful Hannah, over here," said the professor, filling the awkward pause. "But I agree: decide tomorrow. Right now, if you're sure you don't want a ride, Brad, I'm for bed."

"I'm sure. Good night, Professor Harrison; thanks." Brad dipped his head to the others when the professor had left. "Mrs. Harrison, ladies."

"What a nice day," Suzanne said, turning to Mrs. Harrison after Brad had gone. "Thank you."

"Why, you're very welcome, dear. Now, are you sure you have everything you need? Extra blankets? It's so chilly now!"

"You asked that last night, Mom," said Gillian, impatient for everyone to go to bed, for the wind had risen and the storm seemed to be coming on faster now.

Mrs. Harrison laughed. "Why, so I did. Once a mother . . . Well, good night, girls. Lock up when you're through down here, okay?"

"Okay," Suzanne called after her. Then she turned to Gillian. "You're jumpy. You all right?"

"Sure, I . . ." There was a rumble of thunder. "Look, Suze," she said. "You go on up to bed, okay? I've got to go out."

Suzanne gave her an odd look. "I think you're crazy." She put her hand on Gillian's arm. "Should you really go out on a night like this? It can't be safe."

"It's fine," Gillian snapped. "I'll be fine." She pulled away. "Suze . . ."

"I know, I know. You're in a hurry, and you can't

147

tell me anything. But tomorrow," she called after her softly, "you and I are going to have a long, long talk."

It still wasn't raining very hard when Gillian made her way down to the shore, trying to ignore that she'd forgotten to put on rain gear and that she knew very well it was foolish to take a boat out in a thunderstorm. But she was worried about waking her parents with the car, and about bushwhacking into Lark and Jackie's camp from where she'd have to park it; she didn't want to make an obvious path, and it would be hard not to in the rain and the dark. Besides, the worst of the storm was still a few miles away—three, she figured, counting between a flash and a rumble and dividing by two. If I'm quick . . .

The wind was strong, and she had to row against it most of the way to the inlet.

The storm hit in earnest just as she beached *Sprite*, and she was instantly soaked. The tarp'll be wet, she realized angrily, unless it was in the lean-to; why didn't I try to find a dry one? And some rope; was there any extra rope with it? A lot of good I'll do if I can't make the tent dry.

She crashed through the underbrush, not trying to be quiet; there was so much noise now that it didn't matter anyway. All she could think of was Lark and Jackie, huddled in the tent, trying to avoid leaks, wet and maybe frightened.

A faint glow greeted her from the small clearing, and to her astonishment, Lark was outside with a lantern, wrestling with the extra tarp, which didn't seem very wet, so perhaps it had been in the lean-to after all, or under something. Lark had already tied one corner of it to a tree and was doggedly trying to secure the other corner on the same side to form one edge of a temporary roof—just as I would have done, Gillian thought, proud of her.

"I'll get that," she shouted above the wind.

Lark grinned; she looked exhilarated, happier than Gillian had ever seen her. "You always come just in time!" she shouted.

"Where's Jackie?" Gillian asked when she had Lark's corner of the tarp firmly in her hand.

"Tent. It hasn't leaked too badly yet. Not even a bucketful. Jackie's okay. Scared, but okay."

Gillian nodded and struggled with the tarp; the wind was doing its best to whip it out of her hand, and the rope was slippery and sodden. But finally she was able to tie it down and she and Lark each worked her way along one of the tarp's long sides, their arms stretched high above their heads, pulling the tarp over the tent.

The rope on Lark's corner of the other short end just reached the branches of a tree. Gillian saw that the rope on her own corner would extend down to the trunk of a thick laurel bush at her own corner.

"Wait!" Gillian shouted. "Slope. Your side. Back. Me—higher."

Lark dipped down, tying her rope to a low branch. Gillian stretched and tied hers as high as she could reach, as she'd done at the other end, so that the tarp was fastened higher in front than in back, and the water ran off behind the tent as from a peaked roof.

"Thank you!" Lark shouted, her hair whipping around her face.

Gillian mouthed "You're welcome," but she'd already picked up a heavy flat stone and was hammering stakes; the wind had rocked the tent a bit, pulling several of them partway up. Lark watched, then found a similar stone and did the same, working around the other side of the tent.

"Won't you come in?" she said formally to Gillian, retrieving her lantern when they met at the door, and Gillian, laughing, answered, "Don't mind if I do."

Jackie and Lady were on the piled-up sleeping bags in the middle of the tent, with a flashlight glowing nearby and a half-full bucket of water to one side. Jackie was curled up next to Lady, his arms tightly around her. When Lark came in, he whimpered, and she knelt beside him, saying, "It's all right, punkin, it's all right. We've fixed it so it won't leak anymore." She dumped the water outside, then zipped the tent door shut. "We've fastened the tent down tight again, too; that's what the banging was. I'm sorry if it scared you. That big plasticky cloth," she said to Gillian, "was the only thing I could think of to put over the tent when it leaked. I guess that was right, huh?"

"It sure was. It's just what I would have done."

Lark stood up. "I'll get you a towel." She rummaged near the sleeping bags and threw one of the Harrisons' blue ones to Gillian. Then she shucked off her shirt and shorts. She was so thin Gillian could see the shadows of her ribs in the dim light as she draped a second blue towel around herself. She rummaged again and came up with a blanket—also the Harrisons'—which she put around herself and Jackie. When Gillian, who was too cold to be self-conscious, had gotten rid of her wet shirt and the long white pants she'd worn to the theater, and dried herself off a bit, Lark opened the blanket for her, too. They all huddled together in the middle of the tent, listening to the rain.

"You go to sleep now, punkin," said Lark, rocking Jackie. "Lark's here, Gillie's here, Lady's here, and we're all safe and warm." She switched off both flashlight and lantern and began to sing softly, lullaby words to a tune Gillian had never heard. It was quietly soothing, and Gillian soon found herself nodding. She knew she should get back as soon as the storm ended, but it didn't seem to be ending just yet, and she was very, very tired, content to sit there in the dark tent listening to Lark's soft soprano accompanied by the rain and by the thunder, which was now moving slowly away.

When she woke, the sun was shining and the tent was warming rapidly; Jackie, inside a sleeping bag now, was fast asleep next to Lady, and Lark was nowhere to be seen. Neither were Gillian's clothes.

Quickly, Gillian fastened last night's towel securely around herself and went outside; suppose Lark, thinking Gillian was there to look after Jackie, had run off again? She'd been so exultant last night, so unlike herself.

But she was there, in the big shirt again, serenely lighting the stove and filling the camp kettle with water from one of the bottles Gillian had brought the night they'd made camp. Gillian's clothes were drying on one of the tent ropes.

"I thought you might like some coffee," Lark said when Gillian came out of the tent.

"I sure would." Gillian picked up the small jar of instant. "But you're almost out."

"Doesn't matter. I don't drink it much."

"I'll get you more. Water, too. Milk? Bread?"

151

"Everything," Lark said ruefully. She dug in the shirt's pocket. "I've got some money left." She held out a couple of crumpled bills.

Gillian pushed her hand away. "You can pay me later. When you're sorted out."

"You've been too nice to me."

"Shut up. And thank you," she called, going back to the tent, "for drying my clothes." Then she thought of having to go home, and of the time. But it was barely 5:30, her watch said; if she drank the coffee quickly, she might be able to get back before anyone was up.

"I like it here in the early morning." Lark spooned coffee powder into two tin cups. "I never knew morning could be any good." She tossed her hair back. "My mother named me Lark," she said, watching the kettle and the flame, "because larks sing in the morning, and she heard one, she told me, when I was born. It was merry and hopeful, she told me." Lark lifted the kettle off the camp stove and poured water carefully into the mugs. "I liked having you here last night," she said shyly, handing one to Gillian.

Gillian took it silently, and waited while Lark poured hers. Her clothes were still damp, so she kept the towel on when they took their mugs down to the shore with Lady, who had come out of the tent when they'd begun talking, and they sat on a rock next to *Sprite*, drinking coffee and watching the sky brighten.

Sixteen

THE SKY HAD TURNED blue and cloudless by the time Gillian rowed home. She stepped into a silent, sleeping house, managed to get upstairs without waking anyone, and went to bed.

When she got up again, the day was well underway for everyone else. Suzanne had gone to hunt for wildflowers, the usual note said; the professor was working on his book, and Mrs. Harrison was on the porch with her field painting.

Gillian fixed herself two scrambled eggs with three pieces of toast, and joined her mother on the porch.

"That was quite a storm last night," said Mrs. Harrison as Gillian sat down at the table they sometimes used for meals. "Did it keep you awake?"

"A bit." Gillian spread a generous layer of jam on her toast.

Her mother squeezed some more zinc white onto

153

her palette. "Remember," she said, "when we first came here? We were all so nervous about storms." Mrs. Harrison laughed. "Storms! Margie and I used to lie awake listening to every rustle in the woods. Remember that?"

"Yes. You don't do that now, though, do you?"

"Heavens, no. And I slept through most of the storm last night, too. Not as soundly, though"—she pushed some of the white to one side with her palette knife and mixed it with a blob of bright blue—"as you slept this morning. Suze said you were hardly breathing when she got up. She was up long before me; said she was impatient to get outside."

"Suze is a morning person. Besides, she loves it here. Poor deprived city kid." Gillian put jam on another piece of toast, and ate more egg.

"Gillie." Mrs. Harrison put down her palette, laid a piece of waxed paper over it, and joined Gillian at the table. "It's none of my business, but how are you and Brad doing? You seemed more relaxed together yesterday, but something still seems not quite right. And he called a while ago to say he won't be able to go to the beach, but I took the liberty of inviting him for dinner . . ."

"Sleeping Beauty, as I live and breathe!" Suzanne came onto the porch in pink shorts and a matching T-shirt, carrying a huge bouquet of daisies and a coffee can full of wild strawberries. "Top of the morning, Gillie—well, bottom, really." She peered at Mrs. Harrison's painting. "I wish I could do trees like that," she said wistfully, then held out the flowers and the coffee can. "For you, madame. With my thanks for this weekend."

"Suzanne, what lovely daisies! And what a won-

154

derful lot of berries. I don't know how you have the patience. I love picking strawberries, but those tiny wild ones are so hard to handle! Why don't we have them for lunch? Or do you have plans for them?"

"I saw some rhubarb outside," Suze said, "so I wondered if I could make a pie. A thank-you pie. May I?"

"That would be lovely, dear. I think the rhubarb's still okay." Mrs. Harrison glanced from Suzanne to Gillian. "You girls are on your own for today, I guess, until Brad's through working. I'm determined to finish this painting. The Sunday papers are in the living room. There's *The New York Times*, Suze, as well as the Providence *Journal*."

"Oh, good!" said Suzanne. "Sunday wouldn't be Sunday without the *Times*. By the way, when should I do the pie?"

"Anytime you want. Margie and Peter have to rehearse, so they won't be coming to dinner, although they said they'd try to make it at least some Sundays. But we can have the pie at lunchtime, midafternoon, dinnertime—anytime. Dinner is around six, at least that's when I told Brad to come."

"Anytime's okay with me," Gillian said quickly. Then, realizing that she wanted to make sure she had a chance to get bread and milk for Lark and Jackie, she said, "Well, maybe dinnertime, after all."

"Good," said Suze. "That gives me ages." She stretched luxuriously. "Right now I'm going to be lazy and read the paper. Are there funnies in the *Journal*? I don't remember."

Mrs. Harrison laughed. "Here we get this girl the *Times* and she wants funnies!"

"Oh, I want the *Times*, too, Mrs. Harrison, but I have to work up to it slowly."

155

"The *Journal* will be fine, then; it has lots of funnies."

"Great! Coming, Gill? Can we put the flowers in water for you, Mrs. Harrison?"

"I'll be there in a minute," Gillian said as her mother handed Suzanne the daisies.

When Suzanne had left, Gillian went over to her mother and said quietly, "Mom, it really is okay about Brad and me. We've pretty much decided just to be friends, that's all. He's going with a girl named Michelle. She's away now, but . . ."

"Oh, Gillie!" Mrs. Harrison reached for Gillian's hand. "I'm so sorry, darling, I . . ."

"It's all right, Mom, really. I'm glad about Michelle. I like Brad much better as a friend."

Mrs. Harrison looked skeptical. "I'm here, you know," she said, "if you want to talk about it. Maybe we shouldn't invite Brad over so much."

"No, that's fine. I like seeing him."

"But, Gillian . . ."

Gillian stooped and kissed her mother's cheek. "It's really okay, Mom." And she went quickly to join Suzanne, who was sprawled out on the living-room floor in an ocean of newspapers.

At around three, Suzanne decided to make her pie, so Gillian, saying truthfully that she had an errand, took Peter's station wagon to the supermarket, which was open on Sunday afternoons. She figured she could just manage to keep Lark and Jackie in basic food supplies with her allowance if she was careful; it wasn't as if she had to buy other odds and ends, like light bulbs and furniture polish. She'd have to be careful to keep

156

gas money out, though, but luckily Peter had left her with nearly a full tank.

Gillian avoided the runaway pictures in the supermarket lobby and went quickly inside, where she selected milk, cheese, bread, margarine, oranges, bananas, apple juice, peanut butter, jelly, baloney, mustard, tuna fish, mayonnaise, and cookies. She also bought toilet paper, a small bottle of liquid laundry detergent, some regular kibble for Lady, who was almost finished with the special food, a coloring book and crayons for Jackie, and a paperback novel for Lark. Choosing that was hard, but she finally found one about a woman pioneer; even if Lark doesn't like that sort of thing, she reasoned, it's close enough to what she's doing now to interest her.

That left her with almost nothing till Wednesday, allowance day. But at least she didn't need anything for herself.

She loaded the groceries into the station wagon and drove to the overgrown dirt road that led partway down the peninsula. A car was coming, so she drove past the road and turned around in a driveway about a quarter mile away. This time there was no one in sight, so she went down the dirt road till it became impassable. She pulled the wagon into the underbrush as far as she dared, and lugged the bags on foot, being careful to disturb the brush as little as possible and taking a deliberately circuitous route to Lark's camp.

But no one was there.

Stunned, she stood in the field, her eyes scanning the woods. Maybe they're swimming, she thought, and ran to the shore.

157

There was no sign of them.

Maybe they'd heard the car and hidden.

But they didn't answer her calls.

Well, there's no reason why they can't go for a walk, she said to herself. Or maybe they're getting more vegetables.

But she was sure Lark would do that only at night, and besides, she'd asked her not to.

Gillian put the perishables in the cooler and left the other things in their bags beside it, cursing herself for forgetting to bring water. I should figure out how to get ice, too, she thought. Maybe tomorrow I can buy some and row it over, when Suze is gone and Mom and Dad are both busy.

But it was getting complicated, more than she'd expected.

The pad of paper and a pencil were in the lean-to; Gillian scribbled Lark a quick note:

Hi,

Hope you're okay. Groceries and other stuff in bags and in cooler. Forgot water. Will try to bring it and ice tomorrow. Don't drink lake water. Suze leaves tomorrow so I'll be freer.

Take it easy and be careful.

Gillian

She took another route back through the underbrush to avoid making a path to where she'd left the car.

Brad was at the cabin when she arrived, helping Suzanne with the pie. "Peace," she said, walking through the kitchen. "Have fun, my children."

158

They looked up quizzically, and Brad followed her, grasped her shoulder, and propelled her back to the table, plunking her down in a chair. "That's better," he said. "We've just been talking about you."

"Oh?" Now that she was sitting down, Gillian was very conscious of how tired she was. She wanted only to go to her room and read, maybe sleep.

"Yes." Suzanne sat down opposite her. "You. We're worried about you."

"Nothing to worry about," said Gillian.

"Look," said Brad, "we're probably the closest people to you in the world, except for your family. And we all know one can't tell one's family everything."

"Or one's friends," said Gillian tiredly. "As I've tried to explain. Look, I appreciate . . ."

"Gillian," Brad said firmly, taking her hands, "come on. You're hiding something, and whatever it is doesn't seem to be a good thing. It's making . . ."

Gillian wrenched free; she couldn't think of any other way to avoid a confrontation. "Please," she said, shoving her chair back and getting up, "leave me alone!" She ran out of the room, leaving Suzanne and Brad staring after her.

An hour later, when she was almost asleep, there was a timid knock on her door, which she forced herself to ignore. In a few minutes, it came again—and then a third time, so she stuffed her pillow against her mouth and mumbled "Go away."

But the door opened anyway, and Suzanne sat down on Gillian's bed, putting a hand on her shoulder. "Brad and I were just trying to help, don't you understand? I'm sorry if we've annoyed you—if I have, by asking so many questions. And I'm sorry if I shouldn't have talked to Brad about it, but I've been very worried. For what it's worth, he brought it up, I didn't."

Gillian rolled over onto her back. "For the last time," she said, "what I'm doing or not doing has to be no one's business but mine. I know it drives you crazy, since we've always told each other everything. It drives Brad crazy, too. Look, I know I can't talk to him about it, and I think maybe I could talk to you, but not now, not yet. I don't dare, Suze."

"Are you sure it isn't drugs?"

"Oh, God." Gillian realized she was about to laugh, and she knew if she let herself, she'd have trouble stopping. So she choked the laugh back and said, "No. It's not drugs. It's not booze. It's not a girl. It's not a boy. Not in that way, anyhow."

"What way, then?" Suzanne asked quietly.

Gillian stared at her, realizing she'd given something away even as she'd tried to be evasive.

Suzanne got up and went to the window. "You said you were helping someone. Maybe you'd help better if you had help yourself."

Without warning, Gillian felt herself burst into tears. She flung herself back onto her stomach and buried her face in the pillow again.

In a second, Suzanne's hand was on her shoulder. "Oh, Gillie," she said softly. "Gillie, Gillie, Gillie. What is it? You really can tell me. Please. It's tearing you apart, tearing us apart, too. Don't do this to us, Gillie. We have to face things together, don't we?"

With a great effort, Gillian controlled her sobs, turned over, and sat up. Suzanne reached behind her to the bureau and handed Gillian the box of tissues Gillian kept there.

Gillian carefully blew her nose. "I guess it *is* tearing us apart, isn't it?"

Suzanne smiled ruefully. "Well, let's just say it hasn't been exactly great having you sneak out at night when we aren't going to be seeing each other for about six weeks, and not for months after that."

It was as if a knife had gone into her, shocked her into realizing she was hurting the one person she least wanted to hurt, ever. Gillian threw her arms around Suze and held her close. "I'm sorry, Suze," she said miserably, trying not to cry again. "I'm really sorry. You're right. It's not fair to us, or to you." And then, in as few words as possible, Gillian told Suzanne about Lark and Jackie.

Suzanne was quiet for a long time when Gillian had finished, and she gripped Gillian's hand even more tightly than she'd held it while Gillian had been talking.

"It's a terrible risk," Suze said finally. "A terrible, terrible risk. I mean, you're not a psychiatrist, you're not a social worker; she's got to be a little crazy, Gillie, and she's got her brother . . ."

"He loves her. She loves him, even though she won't admit it. She wouldn't do anything to hurt him."

"I'm sure she wouldn't mean to, Gillian, but . . ."

"Suze, if I turn her in, if I go to the cops or something, she'll try to kill herself again. I'm sure she will."

"Yes, but what's the alternative? What are you going to do?"

"I'm not sure. I'm really not. Maybe help her get to her aunt's, if she finally makes up her mind to go. She seems to be working up to it. At least if she does that, Jackie will be okay."

"What if her aunt doesn't want him?"

"Lark thinks she will. Probably."

"But what if Lark's wrong?"

"I don't know. I don't know much of anything. I just know I've committed myself to them, somehow, and I can't betray them."

"What if they betray you? Lark's the one who read your diary, right? So she knows you're gay."

"Yes."

"But, Gillian, suppose she tells? Suppose something happens and she gets mad at you or just spiteful and she tells—I don't know—the cops or someone; her aunt. You know what it'd look like then to most people, especially if you've taken her all the way to New Hampshire—spent nights with her, maybe, too!"

Gillian realized she hadn't thought of that, not seriously, anyway. Surely Lark had been kidding, as she'd been herself, about blackmail. She couldn't imagine Lark's betraying her, unpredictable though she was. But even if it was foolish to ignore that possibility, she knew she couldn't let it stop her or make her hesitate.

"You know that I don't want being gay to run my life," she said quietly. "And I don't ever want to be a coward just because someone might find out."

"I don't either, Gillian, but . . ."

"I have to do this, Suze. Call it a test, sort of. I haven't thought of it that way, but maybe it is one. Do I have the guts to do it—that kind of test. Besides, if I want Lark to trust me, I have to trust her, too. I have to trust her not to betray me, not to—to accuse me of anything."

"You've only just met her. She's a street kid."

"She is not a street kid. But if she were, it wouldn't matter any more than my being gay matters. She's sweet and scared and lonely, and the bottom line is that I can't desert her. I can't let a risk to me, real or imagined, stand in my way. Period."

Suzanne sighed. "I think," she said slowly, "that you're very wonderful and very foolish at the same time. And even aside from the risk to yourself, I think you're wrong not to get help. Suppose you went to some social worker, in confidence, and at least talked it over? Maybe the social worker could tell you what to do. You wouldn't have to name names."

"It's too chancy. People are looking for Lark and Jackie. I'd have to describe them, at least some, and there'd be questions. Someone would be bound to figure out who they are."

"Well, what about telling your parents, then? Your mom loves kids; your dad's a sociologist; they're nice people, Gillian. And smart, too. Maybe they could think of something."

"That's chancy too, Suze. I'm sure they'd say I should go to the authorities, turn them in. And if I didn't, my folks might, thinking they were helping. Besides, it's our cabin Lark broke into; it's some of our stuff she and Jackie are using. I don't think my folks would love that idea a whole lot."

"Yes, but when they understood why . . ."

"You know it's still risky. Suze, it's a *life* we're talking about. Suppose Lark's reaction to my telling her that I'd arranged for her to get help was to kill herself?"

"Maybe she's bluffing about that."

"That scar on her wrist is no bluff."

"Okay. Then—I'm sorry to be so harsh—but what if she kills herself anyway? What if you *don't* turn her in, get help for her, and she kills herself? Can you live with that? What's the end going to be, Gillian? What are you going to do with her, say in the fall, if she sticks around that long?"

Gillian hesitated. "I don't know," she admitted at last. "I think I'm buying time now, trying to show her it's okay to live, that people can care about each other. Maybe I will have to go to someone in the fall. But it seems to me that a person like Lark can take help better from a friend she trusts than from some stranger of a social worker."

"You're not qualified, Gillian; she's sick! She's got to be! And she's got a child with her. Suppose she hurts him?"

"She'd never hurt Jackie. I told you she loves him; he's the only thing she does love. As long as he depends on her, I don't think she'll do anything rash—unless someone tries to turn her in." Gillian sat up. "I know I'm taking a chance, Suze. But I've thought a lot about it, and I don't see any other way. I've got to help her trust me, like I said. Maybe if she finally trusts me I can get her to agree to get help. But it's too soon now; she's too—too fragile."

Suzanne shook her head. "I know you well enough to know you're going to do what you think you should do, anyway. But I can't agree with you. I think you're wrong, and I know that hurts you, and I'm sorry. But I can't lie to you and say I agree when I don't. I'm scared for you and I think you're making a terrible mistake."

Gillian felt cold inside and outside; it was as if she were turning to ice, quickly and mercilessly. She choked down sarcasm, choked down anger and more tears, and regret. "Please swear," she said to Suzanne in as steady a voice as she could muster, "that you won't say anything about this to anyone. That includes Brad, because he said he thought whoever broke in here belongs in reform school, and because Lark has stolen food from the farm. He'd be the first, I'm afraid, to go to the police."

"Don't be ridiculous, Gillian; of course I won't say anything."

"But you think it's terribly wrong, what I'm doing."

"Yes, I do. But that's as far as it will go. I don't think there's anyone," she went on, "*anyone*—who'd agree with what you're doing."

"You're probably right," Gillian admitted reluctantly. "And that's probably got something to do with my not telling anyone. But I still think—no, I *know*—that I have to go on helping Lark, at least until Jackie's taken care of and at least until she trusts me more. Maybe then she'll be more reasonable about herself. I can't plan it all out beforehand because I don't know what's going to happen next. But I think you'd agree with me, if you knew Lark. If I didn't believe that what I'm doing is right, I wouldn't do it and I would ask for help."

Suzanne put her hand on Gillian's arm. "I know that, Gillie. I know that very well. And I also know you must feel very much alone. I do understand that much, and I ache for you. I love you, no matter what. But I'm very, very scared for you."

Seventeen

DINNER THAT NIGHT was difficult, but it helped a bit that Brad was there, even though he kept giving Suzanne covert glances, as if trying to ask if she'd found out anything. Everyone made a fuss about Suzanne's pie, which also helped, and after dinner Suzanne got Brad to go home. "I just told him we wanted to be alone," she said to Gillian, joining her on the shore after he'd left, "and I said you'd talked to me and that he shouldn't worry. Really. That's all I said."

"Thank you," said Gillian, kissing her.

But she still felt a barrier between them, and despite the fact that she told herself it didn't matter that Suzanne disagreed with what she was doing—disapproved of it, thought it was wrong—it was hard not to let that hurt, or sway her.

That night they held each other in Gillian's narrow bed, each trying to soothe the other wordlessly, but

Gillian was glad when morning came, and there was packing to do, and Suzanne's bus to catch.

They didn't talk much on the way to Providence either, even though Gillian's parents didn't go with them. "August," Suzanne whispered when they hugged as the bus began loading. "We still have August to look forward to. Good luck till then. Please, please, be careful."

And then she was gone.

When Gillian got back to the cabin, feeling ragged and incomplete, there was a police car in the driveway, and she wished instantly that she'd gone straight to the inlet. She turned to leave, but her mother hailed her anxiously from the door. "Thank goodness you came right back. I said I thought you would, but then I wasn't sure."

"What's up?"

"That youth officer is here again. He wants to talk to you."

Something twisted in Gillian's stomach, but she put on a calm face and followed her mother into the living room.

Officer Dolan was sitting on the sofa; he stood as soon as they came in. "Hello, Gillian," he said, and then, like a dismissal, "Thank you, Mrs. Harrison."

As if it had been prearranged between them, Gillian's mother went back into the kitchen and closed the door.

Officer Dolan gestured to Gillian to sit down. "Now," he said, "about those kids you've been seeing. Your mother says she still hasn't met them, but she thinks you must have seen them again. Susan and Larry, right?"

Gillian nodded uncomfortably, the twisting feeling still in her stomach. How many times had she actually said she'd seen them? She couldn't remember. Suppose the police had caught Lark and Jackie, and Officer Dolan was leading her on? But why would he bother?

"You find out their last name yet?" the policeman asked, taking out his notebook.

"They never said."

"And you still don't know where they live?"

"Right."

Dolan wrote something down. "Can you give me a description? I know you don't want to rat on friends, but you haven't known these kids very long, have you? We need to know if they could be involved in the break-ins we're investigating."

"What break-ins?" Gillian managed to ask. "Or do you just mean ours?"

"No, there've been a couple more, and the Finnegans' farm has been losing vegetables pretty regularly. We think your new friends might be responsible, might be runaways, trying to get along. That's not so bad. It'd be more sad than anything else, and we'd want to help them. But the last thing stolen was pretty valuable, a VCR from a summer cabin just a mile or so from here."

"They're not runaways," Gillian told him, keeping her voice steady.

"Do you know that for sure? You said you don't know where they live."

"Yes, but I'm sure they live around here someplace. For the summer." Gillian walked to the window and looked out over the lake; why was her mind working so slowly? "I think maybe they're staying in a camper.

168

You know, an RV. Before they move on. I think they're leaving pretty soon, actually."

"Then you wouldn't mind describing them to me."

What had she said they looked like? At first, Gillian couldn't remember. Then she did, or thought she did, and she said, "Susan's pretty fat. Brownish hair, I think, and . . ." What goes logically with that, she wondered, and isn't like Lark? "She has a sort of pale complexion and—and lots of freckles. She's nice. Very nice. She knows a lot of jokes; she made me laugh a lot . . ."

"Um." Officer Dolan scribbled in his notebook. "And the boy?"

"He's good-looking." Gillian was pretty sure she'd told someone that—or had someone suggested it to her? "He's got brown hair, too, but he looks—um—much healthier than his sister."

"Build? Fat like her?"

"No. No, he's sort of average."

"Anything else?"

"Not that I can think of. Oh—Susan's about my age, I guess, and Larry's older. I think he said he was in college . . ." Careful, Gillian, she said to herself. Next he'll ask where, and that's traceable.

"Where?"

"I don't know," Gillian answered. Too quickly?

"You sure you don't know their last name?"

"Yes."

Officer Dolan raised his eyebrows and gave her a long look, which she tried to meet without flinching. Then he snapped his notebook shut. "Thank you. We're going to be doing some careful looking around," he said casually. "You could save us a lot of trouble if you could tell us where your friends are. If they're here with their parents, and if they're as nice as you say, maybe there's nothing wrong; maybe it's someone else who's stealing. On the other hand, they could be trying to use you as a cover. You wouldn't want to get into trouble yourself, would you?" He stood up and stepped closer to her, looking down at her sternly. She noticed how stubbornly his square jaw was set, as if he could be severe to a kid if he felt it was needed. She hoped Lark and Jackie would never meet him; even though there was still kindness in his eyes, there wasn't as much as on that first day.

"Your mom," he was saying, "tells me you've gone out a couple of times lately without saying where. She says that you've been secretive, not like yourself."

"I'm seventeen," Gillian said angrily. "I don't always tell people where I go."

"My kids are nineteen and twenty, but they've learned that even adults say where they're going and when they'll be back. For their own safety, and to keep people from worrying."

Gillian returned his gaze steadily, but remained silent.

Officer Dolan sighed. "I'll be going. You think of anything you want to tell me, you let me know." He opened the door to the kitchen. "I'll just be off now, Mrs. Harrison."

Gillian turned away as he left, but she stood at the foot of the stairs, trying to hear what he and her mother were saying. Their voices were too soft, though, so she went up to her room and quietly closed the door.

Not long after that, Mrs. Harrison went out, and Gillian decided she should take a minute to make a quick call to Dr. Morelli about Lady before going to the inlet; she was still sure that if the police had found Lark and Jackie, Dolan wouldn't have questioned her the way he had.

"Still nothing," Dr. Morelli said. "I think you could begin to arrange for someone to take Lady permanently, if you can't keep her yourself. How's the paw?"

"It seems better. How long should the bandage stay on?"

"It can come off anytime now. No need to bring her in, unless the wound looks funny. Good luck with her," Dr. Morelli added.

Gillian thanked her and hung up. She left a note saying she'd gone for a row, and took *Sprite* out on the lake, making her way by a roundabout route to the inlet. By the time she'd beached the boat, she'd begun to worry again, and she'd thought of a whole list of things that could have happened to Lark and Jackie; she cursed herself guiltily for not having gotten up extra-early to find them.

But Lark was outside the tent, quietly drawing with one of Jackie's crayons. Jackie was building something out of stones a few feet away, and Lady was chewing a stick. Lady got up, tail wagging, as Gillian approached, and Lark stood, putting down her drawing. "I got your note," she said. "I'm sorry you were worried. We were getting water."

"Oh, my God," said Gillian, realizing she should have thought of that. "I was going to bring you some. Ice, too, for the cooler. I forgot. But I'm so glad you're safe!" Then she asked, alarmed, "Where did you go for the water? Did anyone see you?"

"I don't think so. We went back to that spring. We got lost a couple of times, but I kept close to the shore, and that helped. Lady helped, too. She walks almost okay now. I think we could take the bandage off soon."

"The vet said so, too. I called her, by the way. No one's claimed Lady."

Lark seemed startled. Then she laughed. "I'd forgotten," she said, "that Lady isn't really ours." She looked at Gillian anxiously. "Is everything okay? You seem—I don't know. Tense."

"Sort of okay. No. Not sort of okay." She led Lark a bit farther away from Jackie and told her about Officer Dolan.

"I took the vegetables," said Lark. "I'm sorry. I know you said not to, but I only went at night. Jackie was hungry. He likes carrots a lot. But I haven't done any more break-ins. I didn't take the VCR."

"I didn't think you did. But the trouble is that the police are going to be looking harder for you now, looking for someone, anyway. If they poke around here, they'll find you, and they'll have seen your pictures. They won't believe you're camping for fun."

"Why can't everyone leave us alone?" Lark said in a low voice. "I don't mean you," she added quickly. "But just when everything was going so well. I've almost gotten to like it, living here with Jackie and Lady, with you coming to see us. Jackie doesn't seem to mind the tent anymore. He likes routine, you know? He likes to get up at the same time every day, have the same breakfast. He used to want cereal, but he's gotten used to bread and jelly."

"How's the bread holding out?"

"Okay. We'll need more soon. I wish I could make some."

Gillian smiled. "Do you know how?"

"Oh, yes." Lark smiled back. "Someday when this is all over, I'll make you some."

"I'd like that," said Gillian, hoping that meant Lark was beginning to see a future. She hadn't talked of suicide, or hinted at it, for a few days. Maybe she'd given up the idea. Maybe if she had, Gillian would be able to talk to her about some kind of help.

But then Lark said, sadly, "I guess if the cops are going to be looking harder, Jackie and I better leave. I guess I'd better figure out how to get him to New Hampshire. Laconia. That's where my aunt lives."

Dread swept over Gillian even though she knew she'd been expecting this. But as she forced her mind into clarity, she realized that she welcomed the chance for action, perhaps a resolution, at last. "Lark," she said carefully. "You can't possibly walk to Laconia, New Hampshire."

"No. But Jackie and I could hitch."

"That's dangerous."

"I know. I don't care about that for me. It's only Jackie. But maybe no one would hurt a little boy. Maybe if I made sure the driver was a woman . . ."

"Oh, come on, Lark! If you think you're in trouble now . . ."

"I know, but what else can I do? I can't let the cops find us. And like you said, we can't walk to New Hampshire. Besides, Jackie does need a place to stay. What about winter? He can't stay in a tent in the winter."

"Neither can you."

"Right. And we can't keep depending on you; it's not fair. You're already getting into trouble. The cops'll be watching you soon, too, you'll see. You don't

173

think they aren't going to try to follow you, to find Larry and Susan?"

"I don't know."

"Well, I bet they will. No, we'd better leave, Jackie and I." Lark walked toward the tent. "It's okay," she said. "We'll be okay, hitching."

Gillian watched her, her heart beating wildly. She means it, she thought; she's made up her mind now. And she's right about going; she should get Jackie settled. Herself, too.

But I can't let them hitchhike to Laconia!

"Lark." She was surprised at the sharpness of her own voice. "Wait."

Lark turned.

"I'll take you," she said quickly, so she wouldn't lose her nerve. Despite what Suzanne had said, what her parents, Brad, the "authorities" might think, she was sure there was simply no other solution.

"I've got my sister's boyfriend's car for the summer," Gillian said. "It's a station wagon, a small one, but I think we could get everything in it. The camping stuff, I mean, so we wouldn't have to stay in motels. We could get to Laconia in a day, maybe, but I think we should stick to back roads, so it'll take longer." That'll give me more time, too, she was thinking, to make sure she's not going to kill herself when Jackie's safe. Aloud, she said, "You'll probably get to your aunt's faster if I drive you than if you hitch."

"I can't let you do that," Lark said. "I can't let you take someone's car for me."

"He left it for me to use. And I'll write my folks a note, so everyone will know I'm going to bring it back."

"They'll come after us. Those cops. And they'll put

174

out some kind of bulletin, describing the car. Us, too."

Gillian swallowed. "We could travel at night; we'd be harder to spot. Staying on back roads should help, too."

Lark stood silently for a minute. Gillian sensed she was about to accept, but then she said, "What about the license plate?"

"We could make a fake temporary one. Study how they do the numbers. I've seen unofficial ones, cardboard, in back windows when people have lost their real licenses."

Lark smiled then. "The perfect crime."

"It's not a crime. Not really. And it probably isn't perfect either. But with any luck, maybe it'll get you and Jackie where you want to go."

"I don't want to be there," said Lark. "This is for Jackie."

"Where do you want to be?"

"Nowhere, I guess." Then she whispered it: "Nowhere."

Gillian went to her, put her hands on her shoulders. "If you're nowhere, there won't be any more of those mornings you've just discovered you like. And you won't be able to bake me any bread."

Lark threw her arms around Gillian and clung to her once more like a small, desperate child. "I'm so mixed up," she said. "I guess I don't know what I want anymore. When I'm with you and sometimes when I'm just sitting near the tent or by the lake at night with Lady when Jackie's asleep, that's enough for me—just being, just existing. It's okay, it's fine, it doesn't hurt, and it's peaceful. I don't have to see awful things on TV or hear my father yelling or see my mother looking pained or Jackie crying or anyone

175

hitting anyone. And Lady licks my hand, or Jackie hugs me, or you come and—and smile, and it's okay. But . . ." She loosened her hold and moved away, standing with her back to Gillian and her shoulders slumping. "But you won't be around forever and if I'm—somewhere—I know they'll catch me one day and then I'll have to go back to my parents or maybe even to jail . . ."

"You're forgetting your aunt," said Gillian. "I bet she'll take you in, when she knows how things are. And I don't think anyone's going to put you in jail, even though you did take Jackie with you when you ran away. I think they'd understand why. And who says"—she took a step forward—"who says I'm not going to be around forever?"

"No one is."

"In the abstract, no." Gillian felt as if one wrong word would shatter Lark like a dropped glass ornament. "People die, things happen. No one can be absolutely sure of anything. But I'll be around as long as you want me to be, as long as I can be."

"You mean that now," said Lark. "You feel that now. But you might change. And besides, you'll go to Oregon, and there won't be time for me anymore, and . . ."

"Lark," said Gillian desperately, "you're my friend, remember? It's like you're my little sister, and Jackie's my brother. I love you, Lark, and Jackie, too."

At last Lark turned around. "You love me?" she repeated almost inaudibly.

"Yes. Not—you know, not like I love Suzanne," Gillian added hastily. "There are many kinds of love. Friends can love each other deeply; sisters can. I love my friend Brad, even though he makes me mad some-

176

times, and I love Margie and Peter and my parents. I love them all differently. I know that sounds like a lot of people, but there's room for you and Jackie. I care what happens to you, and I think I always will."

"I don't think I've ever loved anyone," Lark said softly, "at least not for a very long time. Except I've been thinking maybe you're right about Jackie. But he's just a little kid. I'm still not sure love's really possible."

"Please believe me, Lark, it's possible. It's okay if you don't think you can feel it yet. I just want you to know how I feel. And I want you to know I'm not going to desert you, or let you go off by yourself with Jackie into goodness knows what."

Lark stood quietly, tensely, for a moment. Then she reached up shyly and touched Gillian's face. "Onion," she said softly.

Gillian felt she could ask it again now. "Will you let me take you and Jackie to New Hampshire? Please? You can decide the rest later."

"I don't—okay."

Eighteen

EVEN SO, GILLIAN wasn't sure what Lark might do. That same afternoon, she withdrew $350 from her savings account, telling herself she'd pay most of it back as soon as they returned; it would be better to have too much money, she reasoned, than too little. She went to the supermarket and tried to think of what they'd need that she hadn't bought yesterday; they could get ice on the way, maybe from a machine, and more milk if they dared go into a store. She bought some more baloney and some cheese and dry soup. On the way to and from the village she hunted for temporary license plates, and when she didn't find any, she drove to a used-car lot and, spotting one there, parked nearby and sketched it quickly in a notebook.

They'd have to be very careful, travel at night as she'd already decided, sticking to back roads as much as possible, and hope that whatever license number they made up didn't belong to someone else the police were looking for.

When she finished her sketch, she drove back to the village and bought a screwdriver, a pair of pliers, and a hammer, partly for taking off the real plate, but also just to have them, in case she and Lark needed tools—or even weapons. She picked up another flashlight and extra batteries, too, and, as an afterthought, two more coloring books for Jackie and a fake bone for Lady. It all took a lot of money, but she still had a reasonable amount left.

She stashed the supplies in the back, under a luggage-concealing device that Peter had; it rolled out like a window shade and would serve to hide everything until she left, as long as her parents didn't notice that it was in place and wonder why. Chances were, she decided, they wouldn't. There wasn't room for the station wagon next to the Toyota, so its parking spot was some distance away; one would have to make a special point of going over to the wagon and looking inside before one would notice that the luggage concealer was pulled out.

Finally she drove to the drugstore, where there were pay phones, and dialed Suzanne's number in New York, even though she knew Suzanne would probably only just have arrived.

But she hung up before anyone could answer, and stood in the booth, her head resting against the phone. It wouldn't be right to give Suzanne the burden of knowing in advance what she was about to do. She'd figure it out soon enough when she heard Gillian was missing—for, of course, Gillian's parents would call her. And she'd worry about it enough at that point. Everyone would.

But Gillian knew that couldn't be helped.

Mrs. Harrison was in the kitchen when Gillian came in, mixing up a cake for dinner, and Gillian weakened for a moment when she saw her, hands floury and brow furrowed in concentration. Impulsively, Gillian hugged her, and like a small child stuck her finger in the bowl to take a dollop of batter.

"Gillian!" her mother exclaimed, but Gillian could see she didn't mind.

In her room, Gillian made a temporary license plate out of cardboard, copying her sketch but using a different number; she attached string to it. Then she sorted her dirty clothes and did two loads of laundry. She went out on the porch and tried to read while the clothes were in the drier, to seem as normal as possible. But the words ran into each other on the pages and in her mind.

Dinner was hard, but she got through it. Harder still was the phone call she got a bit later from Brad; he wanted to come over, and she didn't want to be tempted to confide in him. But he insisted, and she finally agreed to meet him by *Sprite*'s landing place.

She could tell right away that he had something on his mind, maybe something as pressing as what she had on hers.

"I'm not a detective," he began, after barely saying hello, "but whoever's been stealing from our fields stepped on some experimental plants we've been setting out next to the carrot beds. There are more carrots missing, so I guess whoever's been taking them trampled the seedlings on the way. Dad's pretty mad, and so am I." He stood there, looking at her accusingly, as if he expected an explanation.

"That's too bad," Gillian made herself say.

"Darn right it is. Last night I decided to see what I could see, so I stayed out by the carrots for a while. And you know what? I expected some guy, some snotty dead-beat kid playing pranks. I even had a couple of ideas about who it might be. But then this real little kid comes along, a *girl*. She looked about twelve and she also looked scared, but she ran over the seedlings again anyway, a new batch this time, pulled a couple of handfuls of carrots, and took off before I could snatch her. I wanted to get her, I really did, but then I thought of you and your Susan and Larry story—yes, I've heard about that—and how weird you've been acting lately, and I figured I'd run it past you and see what you had to say." Brad stopped and waited, watching her. "Well?"

Gillian tried not to fidget or look as if she knew anything. "Well, what?" she asked in a fakely bright voice, hollow inside.

"Oh, come on, Gill, don't kid around! You must know something!"

She found she was scraping her foot around *Sprite*'s bow, stirring up dirt and leaf fragments, burying them, stirring them up again.

"Are Susan and Larry real?" Brad asked. "Or are they covers for someone else?"

When she didn't answer, he said, "Okay. Okay, that's the wrong tack. Do you know anything about a little twelve-year-old girl who likes carrots enough to steal them?"

"And if I do?"

"If you do, Gillian, can't you at least tell her steal-

181

ing's wrong? Not to mention tramping through newly planted fields. If you don't, I swear I'm going to go to the police."

"Please don't," she said quickly. "It—it's not that simple."

"So you do know her."

Gillian's mind was racing. She couldn't let him go to the police, even though she and Lark and Jackie would be gone by the time he did—or probably would be, assuming he waited till morning. If he did go to them, it wouldn't take much effort, once her parents found her missing, for everyone to put all the facts together and figure out what had happened, at least enough to start a search.

She'd have to tell him, at least tell him something.

"Let's say," she said slowly, "that I know someone who might be the person you're describing. Let's say she's fourteen, not twelve, and has a five-year-old brother she's desperately trying to protect. Let's say she's run away from home because her alcoholic father beats both her and her brother and makes them feel worthless, and let's say she's trying her damnedest to survive. Stealing carrots helps, especially since her little brother loves them, and since they don't have a whole lot to eat."

"And stealing blankets and dog biscuits and VCRs helps, too, right? Judas Priest! Gillian, I . . ."

"Not VCRs."

"Okay." Brad ran his hand through his hair as if trying to soothe his brain. "But what about cops? Welfare? Psychiatrists? Social workers? Teachers, even?"

"No good."

"Why not?"

182

"She's too scared. She doesn't trust people like that."

"Can't that be overcome?"

"It's too risky even to try. To try harder than I have already, anyway."

"Why?"

Gillian hesitated, then said, "Suicide."

"What?"

"You heard me. Suicide. She tried to kill herself."

"Jesus, Gillian! You can't handle this yourself, you need . . ."

"I have to handle it myself," Gillian said tiredly. "She won't accept anything else, and I can't risk her life."

"She's alive now, right? So the first time could have just been for attention."

"I think that's a cliché. It doesn't work for her, anyway. I think she meant it, means it."

"Gillian, you're not God, you . . ."

"I know, Brad. Believe me, I know. But I won't be able to live with myself if I don't go on helping her."

"Saint Gillian, huh?"

She turned away, hurt.

"Sorry." He touched her shoulder. "I'm just worried you've taken on too much. I'm on your side; you ought to know that. The hell with the carrots, and I guess I can always fence in the seedlings. Look, I'm sure I'd be sorry for the kids if I knew them. But—have you told your parents? Suzanne?"

"Suzanne, yes. She feels pretty much the way you do. My parents, no. Not yet. I have to do that at the right time."

"Okay. I hope you do tell them, though, and soon. Maybe they could help." He stood looking at her for

183

a minute, until she was afraid she was going to blurt out the rest of it to him, but then he put his arms around her and held her gently in a brotherly hug that made no demands. "God help you, Gillian," he said. "I sure wish I could. And I sure hope that what you're doing turns out to be worth it."

"So do I," she said emphatically. "So do I."

Gillian's parents were sitting in the living room when she came back in, so she joined them, intending to stay for half an hour or so and then go up to bed.

"Everything okay?" her mother asked. "You look pale."

"Yes, fine. Brad and I just had a difficult talk. But it's fine, it'll be okay." Immediately she regretted saying that much, for of course her mother would think that was the reason why she'd left when she found her missing the next morning. She'd have to remember to mention Brad in the note she planned to leave, and to say he had nothing to do with it.

Mrs. Harrison sighed. "Brad's such a nice boy. Are you sure . . ."

"Not every nice boy is necessarily right for Gillian," interrupted the professor. "She's known him for so long that he must seem like her brother. Right, Gillian?"

"Right," Gillian said gratefully. "He really sort of does."

"Brothers don't make the best boyfriends." Her father peered around his armchair at her. "At least, I shouldn't think they would. Am I right again?"

"You're right again."

"So what I say," he announced, leaning back, "is

184

that maybe breaking up isn't such a bad idea. Even a clean break. It could be hard on both of you, being friends, as your mother told me you were trying to be."

"I still think it's too bad," said Mrs. Harrison stubbornly.

Gillian got up to kiss her father. "Good night," she said. "I'm pretty tired. I think I'll go up and read."

She looked at them both for a moment—her father, lean and, she realized, gray—had that happened without her noticing?—sitting calmly in his chair, his thin, ascetic face crisscrossed with tiny lines, most of them caused by smiling, but some, no doubt, by battling with the statistics he needed for his book; his long fingers intertwined on his lap—and her plump mother, "comfortably round," as Dad called her, her eyes bright blue, perpetually worried and endlessly loving, if not always endlessly comprehending. How could she leave; how could she worry these people who had watched over her, protected her, loved her, since she'd been born?

Because Lark doesn't have parents like mine, she answered silently; because right now I'm the only one who can watch over her and Jackie, and because if my parents knew what I was planning to do, they'd try to stop me and they'd try to get professional help for Lark. And because a human life is more important than anything else, and because something awful might happen to Lark and Jackie if they went to New Hampshire alone.

"Good night, Mom, Dad," Gillian said again, trying to keep her tone light. "I love you."

She turned and headed for the bathroom quickly,

before they'd have time to question her. Their voices followed her, casual, easy, mildly surprised, but nothing more: "Good night, darling"—that was Mom. "Sleep tight."

And Dad: "We love you, too."

Nineteen

GILLIAN BRUSHED HER teeth, composing the note
to her parents in her mind. She went up to her room,
packed, put her overnight case and the cardboard license plate under her bed, and wrote the note. Then
she wrote it again—and a third time. Her first version
didn't say much except that she had to go away to
help someone, but she kept picturing her mother reading it, seeing the fear and pain in her eyes, her be-
wilderment. Her second note, though, said too much;
it mentioned the aunt in Laconia, and Gillian was
afraid Lark and Jackie could be identified from it. By
the time she'd finished the third version, a compro-
mise between the other two, she was exhausted, and
she lay down on her bed without undressing, trying
to forget the note and her parents so she could review
her preparations in her mind, to make sure she hadn't
forgotten anything.

In about an hour her parents came upstairs, and

Gillian lay there in the dark, following the small sounds of their bedtime rituals, watching under her door for the light to go off on the balcony. About an hour after it did, her father's snoring told her he, at least, was asleep, but her mother sometimes took longer, so she waited a bit more, mentally going over the route she planned to take out of Rhode Island toward New Hampshire. After that, she'd have to look at Lark's map. She hoped Lark had taken the tent down by now, had been able to figure out how—at least the weather was clear—and had organized the camp things. But of course she will have, Gillian thought; she's even more anxious than I am to leave.

It'll be fun, she tried to tell herself; she smiled in the darkness, imagining the despondency in Lark's eyes slowly giving way to something more hopeful. She knew she had to kindle that hope if it came, feed it, if she wanted to save her.

Then unexpectedly, with an intensity that staggered her, she longed for Suzanne, for Suzanne's bounciness and laughter and for Suzanne's arms around her. If only they could both take Lark and Jackie to New Hampshire!

Gillian sat up. She realized she was sweating, tense. I can't think of that, she decided; Lark needs me more now than I need Suze. And Suze wouldn't have come even if I'd been able to ask her.

Would she have?

Be your own person, Gillian, she told herself. If you can't be that, you don't have much to give anyone, Suze included. You're just having to do that sooner than you expected, before Oregon.

Well, then, go ahead.

Gillian turned her mind off, bent down, and slid her

overnight case out from under her bed. Cautiously, she opened the door of her room and listened. Her father had stopped snoring; nothing disturbed the peaceful sound of even breathing from her parents' room except the dripping of a faucet somewhere— kitchen, it sounded like. She could turn it off on her way out.

She picked up the note she'd written and crept slowly downstairs, pausing for a moment to listen.

So far, so good. No one moved or spoke.

She slipped into the kitchen and gave the faucet a turn; it was the hot-water one. She should tell her parents about it, so they wouldn't waste electricity heating water no one was using.

As she put the note on the table, she bent to read it again:

Dear Mom and Dad,

Please don't worry when you find this. I'm fine. I've just had to go away, that's all. I'll be back soon, I'm sure.

It has nothing to do with you, or Brad, or Suze. It doesn't have to do with Susan and Larry either; I made them up when I had to say something. I've been helping two other kids, brother and sister, a lot younger than I said Susan and Larry were. They're runaways, and I'm taking them to their aunt's. They think she'll care for them better than their parents. Their father drinks and beats them, and is pretty generally rotten.

I know what I'm doing is risky and I know you'll probably think I should go to the police or someone about them, but I really think I'm doing the right thing. The kids seem to trust me, but they don't seem to trust anyone else.

I should be back in a few days, maybe less. Please tell Peter I'll be very careful with his car. If I get delayed or anything, I'll call you, I promise. Please try not to worry. And remember that I love you.

Please trust me.

Love,
Gillie

When she'd finished rereading the note, Gillian took a pencil from the tray of odds and ends in one corner of the counter and scrawled, "P.S. The hot-water faucet down here drips. I turned it off hard, but I don't think that quite did it. Maybe it needs a washer? Thought you'd want to know. Love again, G."

Swallowing hard against the sudden lump in her throat, Gillian eased the back door open and walked down the path to the station wagon. She stowed her suitcase in the back seat and put the license plate under it. She'd keep the real plate on till she picked up Lark and Jackie, to save time. No one would be looking for her before then, she reasoned; it would be safe.

And now came the worst part: starting the car without waking anyone up. She'd parked it so it faced down the driveway, hoping to be able to push it farther from the house before turning on the ignition, for the driveway ran down a slight incline. The car was already in neutral, so she reached in, loosened the emergency brake, and pushed against the door frame, keeping one hand inside on the steering wheel, as she'd seen people do at gas stations.

At first the car wouldn't budge, so she closed the door and gave it a sharp shove from behind, knowing she was taking a chance; suppose it got away from her and crashed into a tree?

But luck was with her. The station wagon did begin rolling, but slowly enough so she was able to run around and open the door again. She grabbed the wheel just in time to avoid going into some bushes— which, in any case, she realized, wouldn't have made much noise or done much damage.

The station wagon stopped only about a third of the way down the driveway. Still, it was farther from the house than before, and her parents' room faced the woods, not the drive, so maybe they wouldn't hear.

Gillian got into the driver's seat, fitted the key into the ignition, stepped on the clutch and the gas, and turned the key.

The motor caught right away, sounding to her like ten Mack trucks. She slipped the gearshift quickly into first and went down the rest of the driveway to the road, forcing herself not to hesitate or look back.

It was 2:30 a.m. and the main road was deserted. She went as far as she could on the dirt road to the peninsula, then turned the wagon around, to be ready to leave quickly and to make it easier to load. Switching on her flashlight, she parted the bushes to walk to the field, but found Lark, Jackie, and Lady waiting in the underbrush, the camping gear piled neatly nearby.

Lady pushed her nose into Gillian's hand and Jackie, rubbing sleepy-looking eyes, grinned and said, "Hi, Gillie. We going to Aunty's now?"

"Yes." Gillian hugged him, watching Lark over the top of his head.

`Her eyes were smiling and clear, no trace of despair in them.

It took the three of them about thirty minutes to repack the wagon. Everything that didn't fit in the flat luggage space fit under seats and on the floor, except for the sleeping bags, which they unrolled to make a bed for Jackie and Lady on the back seat. They worked fast and in silence; the only thing anyone said was "License plate?" and "Right" when Gillian nearly forgot to change it, and "Okay" when they were ready to go.

Gillian went over the map with Lark, and within ten minutes they were on a fairly main road leading out of Rhode Island into Massachusetts; Gillian had decided they'd probably be safe on main roads till her parents woke up, found her missing, and—probably—notified the police. Normally, her parents would sleep till around eight.

"Can I make noise now?" Lark asked when they reached the highway.

"Sure."

"*Yay!*" Lark cheered, tossing her hair back, and Gillian laughed.

"You? Cheering?" she said. "You amaze me!"

Lark actually grinned. "This is the first adventure I've ever had in my whole life."

"Aren't we going to Aunty's?" Jackie asked from the back seat.

"Yes, punkin, of course we are. But we're going to have fun on the way, aren't we, Gillie?"

"Sure," said Gillian, trying to match Lark's ebullience. But despite having been able to laugh at her cheer, and despite having been delighted by it, Gillian felt tired and drained, not triumphant at all, as she'd

192

expected to feel when they finally got underway. And now she was also worried that Lark's mood would change, as it so often did, or that they'd be spotted despite their precautions.

Still, they had a couple of hours till dawn, till they'd have to start traveling on back roads, and Lark had the map already marked out, at least partway, so they wouldn't have to worry about getting lost.

It took them no time at all to get to the Massachusetts line. It was nearly dawn when they reached Worcester, and they decided to risk a really main highway for an additional hour or so, just to gain more lead time before stopping to sleep.

"I wish I could drive," Lark said when Gillian approached Route 290 at Worcester and traffic began to thicken. They'd given up trying to keep Jackie awake; he was sound asleep by then, curled up in the back with his head on Lady's flank. "You could teach me, maybe."

"No way," said Gillian firmly. "All we need is for someone to stop us and find an unlicensed driver at the wheel."

"I guess you're right. Anyway, you're a good driver."

"Straight A's in driver ed."

"What about other things?"

"B's, mostly," Gillian told her. "A couple of A's in science—biology, whatever I could relate to trees and things like that. What about you?"

"I told you, I'm supposed to be gifted. But I never cared about anything like you care about forestry. That must be nice, though, being in the woods and stuff. I liked camping, more than I've ever liked anything. The world's—cleaner, somehow, outdoors."

"In a lot of places. But, I warn you, not all. You should see what people throw away in national parks." Then Gillian regretted saying that, fearing it would make Lark sad again, but Lark seemed more intrigued than discouraged, so Gillian told her about the national parks she'd hiked in with her family, and those she still wanted to visit or work in.

"Maybe we could do some of that," Lark said, "after we drop Jackie off."

Gillian glanced at her; she seemed serious. Had she abandoned her suicide plan, then, because of the "adventure" of traveling? Or was she just postponing it? "Okay," she said carefully. "Unless your aunt wants you to stay."

"She won't. Where are the White Mountains?"

"New Hampshire." Gillian moved out to pass a truck. "Just north of your aunt's."

"We could go there after we drop Jackie off. Couldn't we? Or do you have to go right home?" Lark looked discouraged again. "I'm sorry. Of course you have to go home. I keep forgetting you have a family. And Suzanne."

"True, I do." Gillian was careful to sound casual. "But remember that I care about you, too. Let's see how it goes, okay?"

Lark nodded vaguely, then pointed out the window. "Route 190's coming up. We could stop there. I bet you're tired."

"I am. But there's noplace . . . Lark." Gillian's eyes were caught by a flash in the rear-view mirror. "Lark, there's a police car."

"Well, don't speed." Lark turned around calmly. Then her face drained of color. "Oh, no, he's coming

194

right at us! But he can't be after us, it's too soon."

"If one of my folks got up . . ."

"But your parents can't have any idea which way we went, Gillian, unless they saw you leave and followed you, and waited around while we loaded the car, and followed us again. They'd have stopped us long before now if they did that. And if they'd been following us, they wouldn't have been able to call the police." She put her hand on Gillian's arm. "Take it easy. You're going too fast."

Gillian slowed, calmed by the logic of Lark's argument, and a moment later the police car swerved into the left lane and sped past.

"Whew!" said Gillian.

Lark smiled, but she seemed tense now.

"I don't want to stop to camp yet," Gillian told her. "But we'd better get off the highway soon. You've got the map, Lark. Where's a good place?"

"There's a road to someplace called Chaffinville," Lark said after studying the map for a few seconds. "From there—a bit beyond it, really—we can get to Route 31, which is the one that goes near that mountain—Wachusett. You said you thought there'd be places to camp around there."

"Right."

"There's the exit," said Lark a minute later. "It must be."

Gillian turned onto the ramp, then drove a few hundred yards down a quiet side road, found a bit of shoulder, and pulled over. "Just for a minute," she said. "I'm a little tired."

"You sleep, then," said Lark. "I'm wide awake; I can keep watch for a while. Here, why don't we change seats? You could curl up more without the steering wheel. It's still early. We don't have to go on right away."

"It's too open here, Lark; we can't stay for long. I'll just close my eyes for a couple of minutes; that's all I need."

"Coffee, then, for when you wake up." Lark reached into the back seat. "It's probably cold now, but there wasn't any thermos. I made some and put it in a mayonnaise jar. I hope it doesn't taste funny. No—when you've slept," she said, when Gillian reached for it.

"This'll do me fine instead." She took a swallow; it did taste funny, but not so bad she couldn't drink it. "Once more," she said, handing the jar back to Lark, "you amaze me."

Then she started the car again.

Twenty

GILLIAN STOPPED A WHILE later in a secluded spot near Wachusett and fell asleep in the driver's seat. When she woke, the sun was shining spottily in her face, interrupted by trees. Lark and Jackie had unloaded the camping gear and were already setting it up near a large oak some distance away. Lady was sniffing around the tree's base, looking as if she was about to dig a hole or hollow out a sleeping place.

"Good morning," said Lark cheerfully when Gillian, yawning, got out of the car and walked stiffly over to them.

"Umm." Gillian picked up a tent stake and sleepily pounded it in.

"Oh, no," said Lark. "I hope you're not one of those people like my mother who's grumpy in the morning."

"Grrr." Gillian pounded in another stake.

"I'd make you some more coffee, but it's really

197

night, the way we're living, and I don't think people like to drink coffee right before they go to bed. Do they? My parents don't. Maybe you should go back to sleep right now. I think Jackie and I can do this by ourselves."

"Don't want you to."

Lark looked amused; well, let her, thought Gillian, shaking out the tent's door flap; do her good.

Lark sent Jackie to the car to feed Lady. "You know," she said conversationally, attaching the tarp's side ropes, "I used to hate getting up in the morning, because there didn't seem to be anything to get up for. And I hated going to sleep at night, because I was scared, I guess. But now—since I've known you, I mean—it's different. I don't mind anything so much." She paused, as if waiting for a response, but went on while Gillian was still trying to think of what to say. "What about you? I bet most people who don't like to get up have different reasons for it."

"I guess some people don't want to get up because they hate their jobs," Gillian said, suppressing another yawn. "Or school. Mostly, though, I think people just like being nice and warm in bed, and feeling lazy. I'm glad you like getting up more now." She pounded in the last stake, then asked casually, moving to one of the back poles, "What were you scared of at night?"

"My father, and . . ." She pointed to her wrist, unbandaged now and almost healed.

"But no longer? You're not scared at night anymore?"

"Not as much. We do the poles now, right?"

"Right."

They raised the tent, then tightened the guy ropes

till its sides were taut. Lark unrolled the two sleeping bags and spread them out inside.

"Jackie and I can double up," she said, then looked around. "He must still be feeding Lady. I'll go get him." But instead she stood there, eyes on Gillian, as if there were something more on her mind. "Did you," she asked finally, "ever want to . . ."

"Kill myself?" asked Gillian deliberately, thinking maybe it would be good to use the words, make them sound as terrifying as they were. "No, I don't think so. I've thought about what it would be like, though, and I've thought that—that maybe it's a good thing that one *can*—you know, if things got unbearable, like if a person were terribly sick with no chance of ever getting better. But no, I never thought seriously about doing it myself. I never thought things were bad enough, I guess."

Lark fumbled with the zipper on one of the bags. "What if everything went wrong? What if Suzanne decided she didn't love you? Or your parents died in a plane crash? Or there was a war or something?"

Gillian hesitated. "Those things would be bad, but there'd still be a chance they'd get better. Or that I'd somehow be able to deal with them. At least that's what I think, what most people think."

"Suicide's a coward's way out?"

"No. No, I . . ."

"Weak way, then." Lark stood up. "I'll get Jackie. The bags zip together—you know that. Maybe we should just sleep on top of them. It'd be cooler, and there'll be more room for all of us."

"Good idea."

When Lark left, Gillian zipped the bags together.

Then she thought about undressing, but decided against it; what if they were found?

Lark came back in a few minutes, leading a very sleepy Jackie, and called softly to Lady, who was lingering outside. "I think we'll be safe here," she said. "There's no one around. But there's one thing, Gillian: do you have an alarm clock?"

"Oh, good grief, no."

"How'll we make sure we wake up at the right time?"

"We'll just have to take a chance, I guess. It gets hot in tents in the daytime. Maybe that'll wake us up." She helped Lark put Jackie, who had fallen asleep again, in the middle of the two bags.

"Or Jackie'll wake us. He's already slept a lot." Lark curled up next to her brother.

Gillian lay down on the other side of Jackie and fell asleep before she could do any more worrying.

Late that afternoon, it was Jackie who woke them, as Lark had predicted, although Gillian was vaguely conscious of heat and smells before then—wax from the tent floor, mostly. When she opened her eyes, Jackie was sitting up, pummeling Lark, saying, "Larkie, I'm hungry! Come on!" and Lark was shushing him.

"It's okay." Gillian sat up, happy, relaxed. She'd dreamed of Suze, a good dream. She watched Lark and Jackie lazily; they looked nice together, the little fair head and the larger, darker one. Their jaws had the same line, she could see, and their noses were proportionately small and pert. "I'm awake."

"Jackie, why don't you and Lady go outside and pee?" said Lark. "Gillie and I will be out in a second, okay?"

"Aren't you going to pee, too?"

"Yes, of course. Later. Shoo!" Lark unzipped the tent's door. "And be quiet," she whispered, fingers to her lips. "We don't want anyone to know we're here. It's a secret, okay?"

"You said I was good with him," Gillian remarked, "but you are, too."

"Not that good. And only when I'm in the right mood. How about peanut-butter sandwiches for breakfast?" Lark asked, rummaging in her pack. "We probably shouldn't take the time to cook anything or make a fire. Maybe later tonight. We'll be farther then. We could cook something for lunch. That dry soup is around somewhere."

"Good idea." Gillian looked at her watch. "It's still afternoon—only five-thirty. We've got a lot of time till dark."

"We should get a start, though, shouldn't we? We're on back roads."

"I think we ought to stay here a while longer before we go out on the roads, even back ones. Till closer to dark. Let's eat first—whoa!"

Jackie came dashing back into the tent, nearly knocking it over, Lady close at his heels. "There was a boy! Fishing. Lady and I found a lake. I didn't drink any, but I'm thirsty. Lady's Band-Aid came off. Lark . . ."

Gillian handed him a small juice bottle, first unscrewing the lid. "Apple juice. That should help." She examined Lady's paw; it looked fine. "Lady'll be okay without her Band-Aid."

"Did the boy see you?" Lark asked.

Jackie shook his head, gulping juice. "I don't think so. And I wouldn't tell, anyway. But there was a man,

201

too. They were on the land, not in a boat, and Lady almost barked."

"Then we'd better get out of here," Gillian said.

"Food." Lark nodded toward Jackie. "He'll get cranky."

"You make some sandwiches and I'll strike the tent. Or the other way around. It doesn't matter."

"It doesn't matter to me either. Here—the bread's near me, so I'll do the food. Besides, you know the tent better."

Gillian unzipped the sleeping bags and rolled them up, then moved their gear out of the tent. By the time she was through, Lark had already given Jackie his sandwich and put out a bowl of kibble for Lady.

"She drank the lake," said Jackie.

"It's okay for dogs. Just not for people." Lark spread more bread with peanut butter while Gillian loosened the guy ropes.

"Why?"

"I don't know."

"Dogs have special things in their spit that kill germs," said Gillian.

Lark looked at her.

"I read it someplace," she said. "I don't know. Maybe it's cats that have that. Don't quote me, Jackie."

"What's that?" Jackie asked, his mouth full of sticky sandwich. "What's quote?"

"Quote is to say what someone else said. If you said 'What a rogue and peasant slave am I,' and then I said it, I'd be quoting you. And you'd be quoting Shakespeare, because he said it first."

"What a *what*?" asked Jackie, giggling.

"Rogue." Gillian tweaked his nose gently. "Shakespeare"—she grabbed at a rope that had just escaped her—"was a man who wrote plays a long, long time ago. He wrote the plays in that big book I brought for Lark, and he said a lot of wise things, so people quote him all the time. Especially my sister, who's an actress."

"I didn't think a forester," said Lark, helping with the tent now that the sandwiches were made, "would quote Shakespeare or . . ."

Lady barked then, silencing them, and a moment later a man and a boy appeared, carrying fishing gear.

"Afternoon." The man touched his cap politely. "That your dog?"

"Yes." Gillian's throat was so dry she had to force the word through it.

"Nice," said the man mildly. He looked at the half-struck tent. "Campin' here long?"

"No," said Lark. "No, we're just going."

"Good thing," the man said. "Woods is closed to campin'. Fire danger. Campground's down the road a ways. But it's closed, too." He smiled. "Don't blame you for pitchin' it here, though. Don't like crowds myself." He regarded them curiously. "You family? Sisters?"

"No," said Gillian quickly. "Well, sort of. She and I"—she nodded toward Lark—"are friends. The little boy's her brother."

"Folks around?"

"No," said Lark, smiling ingenuously, trying, Gillian could see, to charm him. "They finally said they'd let us go camping by ourselves; our families have been camping together for years."

Jackie's eyes widened and fixed on Lark; Gillian put her arm tightly around him. "We've got to head home now, though," she said.

"Umm," said the man.

Now he's going to ask where's home, thought Gillian—but he seemed satisfied, for he touched his cap again, said, "Come along, Malcolm," to the boy, who'd been staring at Jackie, and left.

"Wow," said Gillian. "That was a close one."

"You lied again, Lark," said Jackie accusingly.

"It wasn't a bad lie, punkin. It was like before. I had to lie so he wouldn't get someone to make us go back home. We want to go to Aunty's instead, don't we?"

Jackie nodded, but his lower lip trembled.

"Come on, Jackie." Gillian took his hand. "Let's see if we can skip to the car. Do you know how to skip? And maybe later, while we're driving, you can count cows for us. Okay?"

They drove to another secluded spot, finished their sandwiches, and took turns making up stories for Jackie till nearly dark, when Gillian decided they could risk traveling again. Lark hadn't mentioned anything more about suicide.

"I've been thinking," Lark said when they were almost at the New Hampshire border. "Maybe we ought to dye your hair."

Gillian nearly drove off the road. "Why?" she managed to ask.

"It's you they'll be looking for. Jackie and I have been gone so long I bet no one's really hunting for us anymore. But your parents probably gave the police a description—you really don't think they *won't* have told the police, do you?"

"No," Gillian admitted.

"So if we dyed your hair . . ."

"Black hair doesn't dye," Gillian said shortly.

"Bleach it, then. It's not that I don't like it. But it's just . . ."

"I bet you wouldn't like it if it were red."

"Twenty-ten!" Jackie shouted triumphantly from the back seat, apparently still counting cows, though it was dark now.

"Great, punkin. What do you mean if it were red?"

"That's what black hair turns into when you bleach it. Someone told me that, I forget who; my sister, probably. She knows that kind of thing. Anyway, I don't see myself as a redhead."

"It'd grow out."

Gillian glanced at her. "Do I have to?" she asked, deliberately sounding like a petulant child.

Lark laughed. "No, of course not."

"But for you I should." Gillian sighed. "All right. I'll think about it, if you insist."

"I just thought it would be a good idea."

Lark sounded subdued; she was staring straight ahead at the road. "Hey," Gillian asked, "what did I say? Lark?"

Lark shook her head silently.

There she goes again, Gillian thought. Switching on me.

"It's just," Lark said when they'd been in New Hampshire for sometime and were making a pit stop in the woods near Greenfield—it was very dark now, starless—"it's just that some cop might see the fake license plate and stop us, and he'd have a description of you, and if your hair were different . . ."

"If a cop stops us," said Gillian, spreading a cracker with peanut butter, "he'll ask for my driver's license. And it'll be all over then, hair or no hair."

"You're right," said Lark. "I never thought of that." She grinned. "Good. I like your hair the way it is."

Twenty-one

THEY STOPPED JUST outside Laconia, pitched the tent, and watched the sun come up over a deserted lake's unruffled surface, while they ate the last of the bread and sipped apple juice. "Why should anyone look for us at all?" Lark said, stroking Jackie's hair. He was lying with his head in her lap, breathing quietly, fast asleep. "Maybe no one will. Maybe your folks will let you go; maybe they'll realize you're okay when they read the note, and that you know what you're doing. And they'll just wait, maybe, for you to come back."

"Maybe." Gillian looked out over the water, which was turning from gray to blue in the growing light. Two ducks made a ladder pattern on the surface as they swam silently along the shore.

Lark shifted Jackie on her lap. "I zipped the sleeping

bags together again," she said. "That was nice, all snuggling together."

"Lark," said Gillian, "we've got to make a plan. I mean, we're here now, or almost."

"I know."

"Do you know what street your aunt lives on?"

"Yes. I even know how to find it. Once we get to the center of town, I can find it."

"How big is Laconia?" Gillian asked, trying to remember the size of the dot on the map. "A city?"

"Not really. Biggish, but not big. Not like—oh, not like Providence."

"Just the right size to find a runaway in," Gillian said grimly.

"They won't find us. Besides, we'll get to my aunt's quickly, once we're really in Laconia." Lark stopped.

"How are we going to work it?" Gillian asked when it was clear that Lark wasn't going to say any more. "Do you want me to go with you?"

"No. She might—you know. Tell. You'd get into trouble then, maybe. You could wait for me. I could take Jackie and then . . ."

Lark fell silent.

Gillian tried to keep the anxiety out of her voice. "And then?"

"Well, and then I could come back to you. Except you have to go home." Lark picked up a twig and broke it into little pieces. "So I could go on by myself."

"Where?"

Lark shrugged.

"You're not still . . ."

"I thought I'd tell my aunt I hitched." Lark threw stick fragments into the lake, brushing one or two stray ones out of Jackie's hair. "Or I'll say I came with a friend. I could say I'm going back with the same friend. Then my aunt wouldn't ask questions. Probably not, anyway."

"And will you?"

"Will I what?"

"Go back with the friend?"

Lark moved Jackie carefully off her lap, then stood, struggling to lift him; Gillian got up and helped. "We should go to sleep."

"Lark . . ."

But Lark was already heading toward the tent, Jackie in her arms.

Gillian lay in the dim tent, her eyes stinging in the light that filtered through the canvas; it was very hot. Her watch said it was just after noon.

Should she offer to take Lark to the White Mountains, as Lark had suggested earlier? But what then?

Would Lark try to kill herself if she were alone?

Did she have the means to do it? A razor blade? A knife? Pills?

She rolled over slowly, then snaked herself off the bag, crawling toward Lark's pack—but Lady woke, wagging her tail across Lark's face.

"Umm." Lark rubbed her eyes. "What time is it?"

"Ten past twelve," Gillian told her. "Go back to sleep. We've still got plenty of time. It's hours till dark."

But Lark sat up. "We ought to get to my aunt's in the daytime," she said. "It'll seem more normal." She prodded Jackie. "Come on, punkin. Wake up! Want a swim before we go? Hmm?"

209

Jackie woke up whimpering. "Don't want to go," he whined as Lark led him outside; Gillian followed. "Want to stay here."

"But it'll be fun at Aunty's, Jackie," Lark said, kissing him. "You'll have your own room, I bet, and everything. It'll be great."

"Lady coming, too?"

"If Aunty lets her stay, punkin. If she doesn't, then I'll keep her for you. Or Gillie will, okay? Won't you, Gillie?"

"Sure," Gillian said.

"You coming to Aunty's, too, Lark? You staying there?"

"Punkin, I told you, I can't stay. I can't, Jackie."

So she probably hasn't given up her plan after all, Gillian thought. Lark's words hit her like blows, and she was furious at herself for not searching Lark's pack earlier.

"Gillie coming?"

"No, Gillie can't come. But you're going to get to stay there, in a nice room and everything. And go to school, and have other little boys to play with." Lark hugged him so tightly he protested. Then she took his hand and ran with him, unsmiling, to the lake.

Her eyes, Gillian noticed, were dead again, empty and blank, and that filled her with foreboding.

But she seemed cheerful when Gillian pulled the car up to the edge of a tiny park which Lark said was only a few blocks from her aunt's house. They'd stopped in a small gas station, deserted except for a bored-looking teenage attendant, and Lark had combed both her hair and Jackie's and scrubbed their faces with hot water and soap until they shone.

"Sunday-morning faces," she'd said cheerfully when they'd come out of the ladies' room and climbed back into the car, both of them in the front this time.

"You'll come back?" Gillian asked when she'd driven to the other side of the park and turned off the ignition; Lark opened the car door. "You promise me you'll come back?"

"Yes," said Lark. "Really. And I'll be as quick as I can."

"Okay." Gillian knew she had no choice but to believe her. "I think I'll find a better place to park and then go sit on one of those benches. I don't think I'll be as conspicuous that way."

"Okay. Gillie?" Lark gave Gillian's hand a squeeze. "I don't know what I'm going to do. I mean later. But I really will come back after I leave Jackie. I promise."

Gillian smiled, and squeezed her hand back.

"Jackie, it's time, punkin. Say goodbye to Gillie and tell her thank you."

Jackie looked alarmed and almost ready to cry again. "Want Gillie to come," he said, pouting.

Gillian scrunched away from the steering wheel and took him on her lap. "I can't come right now, Jackie. But I'll write you and Lady lots of letters and I'll come back and visit sometime." She patted his hand. "You promise to be there, okay? So I won't miss you when I come. And then you can tell me all about your new room and everything. Okay?"

Solemnly, Jackie nodded.

"Good boy." Gillian kissed him, and Lark mouthed "Thanks" in her direction.

Then Lark and Jackie got out of the car, put Lady on her leash, and walked away.

"I'll miss all three of you," Gillian whispered, her eyes moist.

She parked the station wagon, bought a newspaper, and sat on a bench in the warm July sun, reading.

An hour later, when she'd read almost every word in the paper, Lark still hadn't returned, so she went back to the newsstand and bought a magazine. But she couldn't concentrate, even though she'd bought it because it had a forest-ecology article in it. Had something happened? Had Lark broken her promise and gone off on her own?

Just as she was getting frantic, Lark arrived. "You must be famished," she said, as if hers had been the most casual of errands. "Aunty gave us lunch, that's why it took so long. Here." She sat down and handed Gillian a thick sandwich, neatly wrapped. "I told Aunty that my kind teacher Miss Harrison would love a roast beef sandwich, and that she might not go to a restaurant because of trying to save money. She doesn't have much money, I said, because she has to pay her old mother's nursing home bills."

Gillian bit into the sandwich eagerly, wondering briefly how she could have been so worried one minute and be so ravenous the next. "What happened?" she asked around a chunk of beef.

"Nothing much. My aunt takes things pretty easy. She was very independent when she was a kid, my mother always said, and like I told you, she's always thought my mother is in a bad marriage. I told her things had gotten worse and that I didn't think Jackie should stay there anymore. And that we'd picked up this dog, and that Jackie loved her. That part was fine; she said she'd take them both, and call my folks to

212

say Jackie was there, and that she'd be willing to keep him—and Lady, but of course my parents wouldn't care about her. Aunty said she'd try to get my mother to come, too, and stay with her. To leave my father."

"And you?"

Lark looked away. "She wanted me to stay. But I said I didn't want to. I told her Miss Harrison and I were going on a trip and that Miss Harrison said I could live with her till I finished school. She asked me a lot about that. I think she believed me, though, in the end. I don't think my mother will catch on, if Aunty mentions it to her, even though I never had a Miss Harrison teaching me and I don't think there's one in the whole school. My mother's never been too clear on my teachers' names and she'll probably pretend she knows who Aunty's talking about because she'd be embarrassed to admit she doesn't. So I think it'll be okay." Lark smiled faintly and spread her arms wide. "I think I'm free!"

"Lark," said Gillian, "shouldn't you go back? I mean, if your aunt wants you to stay, and you like her? Since Jackie's there, and Lady? How was Jackie, by the way, when you left?"

"Sniffly, but okay. He loves Aunty and I think he was glad to be in a real house again. She'll take good care of him."

"Is she married?"

"She's a widow. She's been one ever since I can remember, and she's a lot stronger than my mother."

"About you . . ."

"I can't stay there, Gillian."

"Why not?"

Lark stood up and moved away from the bench. "I don't know. But I can't."

213

"Lark, that doesn't make sense. Please, look, you . . ."

Lark wheeled on her angrily. "It's my life. I can do what I want with it. All my life I've had to do what other people wanted. Now I want to do what I want. It's my life," she repeated softly.

"I know it's your life," Gillian said. "But I don't want to see you throw it away. You're too important, too . . ."

"Oh, come on! I'm not important, I'm not anything. Sure, my aunt invited me. But she didn't really want me there, I bet. Another mouth to feed. I can't ask her to feed three of us, Gillian; Jackie and Lady and me. And I . . ."

Gillian tried not to notice the people who had begun to stare as her voice and Lark's had risen. She touched Lark's shoulder, got control of her voice again, and asked, "What's really wrong, Lark?"

Lark shook her head; her body was rigid, unresponsive.

"Let's get out of here," Gillian said resignedly, realizing Lark needed more time. "Let's go back to that lake, or to another lake. You said something about the White Mountains. Let's go there. Maybe you'll be able to think better outside the city."

Lark remained unmoving, but her shoulders relaxed a little.

"Come on," Gillian said. "The car's over here." She pulled Lark up and turned her toward it, and finally Lark walked with her. Her face was stony, though, and her eyes withdrawn.

Lark remained silent while Gillian drove out of the city and turned north on a secondary road; she'd had plenty of time to study the map. A while after the turn, Lark sighed and said, "I'm sorry. I'm so awful to you. I'm sorry."

"It must have been very hard, leaving Jackie like that."

"I didn't think it would be," Lark said, and Gillian realized she was crying softly. Gillian pulled the car over to the shoulder and put her arm around her.

"I guess I really do love him," Lark sobbed. "I guess I didn't believe that before, even when I said maybe I did. It hurts inside to know I'm away from him. But I can't keep him, Gillian, and he can't stay with our parents. I know it was the right thing, but I . . ." She clung to Gillian, sobbing on her breast while cars sped by and the sun, growing steadily hotter, beat down on the car.

Finally, Lark's sobs eased and she moved away from Gillian, rummaging in the glove compartment for the box of tissues they kept there. "I'm sorry," she said again, after blowing her nose. "I got you all wet."

"Doesn't matter. I'll dry fast in this heat."

"Pretty," Lark said, looking at her. "You're pretty. I've been thinking that, off and on, the whole time. I've felt funny about saying it. But I watched you sometimes. You have such a strong face, but it's gentle and kind."

"You're pretty yourself, you know," said Gillian casually. "People," she said, pulling her head back to give Lark a mock-appraising look, "will come from miles around to see the beautiful Lark . . . but," she added as a truck whizzed by, "I think we'd better get back on the road before someone smashes into us and we both lose our gorgeous looks."

215

Lark giggled, but as Gillian pulled out, she said, "It'd be a lot easier if someone did smash into us. Into me, anyway." ,

"Easier than what?" Gillian asked sharply.

"Than having to decide things. Than dealing with them. Doesn't it make you tired, having to deal with things?"

"No. No, it doesn't. It makes me excited. It can be an adventure, Lark. You like adventures."

"But what if it all goes wrong? It always does."

"It does not always go wrong!"

"It does," Lark insisted. "You'll see. I don't dare feel good about anything for long, because it always gets screwed up if I do. Look at Jackie. I loved him, love him. But I had to give him up."

"You didn't really have to. And you don't have to. You could go back to him right now. Even if you didn't now, you could go back to him anytime, to visit or maybe even to stay."

"Maybe."

Lark stretched, her mood switching again; Gillian sensed it even before she spoke. "Let's splurge," Lark said. "Let's stop somewhere and have a real meal. Let's go off the road to a town and have a big steak before we make camp tonight."

Gillian continued driving around and through the mountains, and Lark's good mood held. Sometimes they sang with the radio, and sometimes they were silent, admiring the spectacular scenery. In a while Gillian felt that she could trust Lark's mood and that underneath it, for the moment anyway, she was no longer despondent. If there's one thing I can try to do

216

for her, she vowed, it's make her see that everything doesn't always turn out badly.

But, dear God, what am I going to do with her?

Not far from Conway, the sky darkened, and soon they were driving through a drenching thunderstorm; Gillian finally pulled off to wait it out. In a while, it settled into a steady rain, and Gillian drove on, wondering how they were going to make camp, and afraid they might have to sleep uncomfortably and unsafely in the car. Then she spotted a small run-down cabin place ahead. Well, why not, she thought. It can't cost much—and when she broached the idea to Lark, Lark answered, "I wanted to say that myself, but I didn't think I could, since you're the one with the money."

The man at the desk was so old he looked shriveled, and if he'd heard about any runaways, he clearly wasn't letting it bother him. "Only one bed," he said dubiously when they both went in to register, but before Gillian could reconsider, Lark said, "That's okay; my sister and I are used to doubling up." She signed her name, unblinking, as Lark Harrison after the man had asked to see Gillian's driver's license as identification, and Gillian, realizing there was no way to avoid it, had shown it to him.

The cabin was tiny, the main part just big enough for a large double bed, a chair, and a bureau holding a TV set, but in a little jog off the back there was an even tinier kitchen and bathroom. "We could cook!" Lark exclaimed, and her enthusiasm was so infectious that after they unpacked the car, Gillian took her out again to a grocery store they'd passed and bought a steak, a package of french fries, some frozen vegetables, salad makings and dressing, and a small chocolate cake. They also bought half a dozen eggs for the morning, more bread, margarine, and juice.

Cooking wasn't easy in the tiny kitchen. They got in each other's way and realized they couldn't broil steak and bake french fries at the same time. "Let's do the fries first," Lark suggested efficiently, "and then we could wrap them up in foil . . ."

". . . if we had foil . . ."

"Well, put them in a pot, then, or maybe a frying pan with a cover, and keep them hot till the steak cooks. Here," she said. "You be in charge of the vegetables and the salad."

The meal was good, though unevenly heated, and they ate it on cracked, unmatched plates at the miniature kitchen counter. After the cake, Lark stretched and announced, "I'm going to take a shower, how about that?"

"And I'm going to take one when you're done," said Gillian, amused and then amused that she was amused. There had been something about watching Lark in the kitchen—she'd looked like a child doing an adult's job, but doing it almost as well as an adult—that had started her smiling, and she still felt warmed by Lark's cheerful mood. "We can wash the dishes in the morning. I bet there's not a lot of hot water here."

While Lark showered, Gillian stretched out on the bed and closed her eyes, listening to the rain drumming on the roof and the shower water drumming inside. She felt exhausted, and she found herself longing for Suzanne again.

She forced her mind back to Lark, and then sat up, alarmed, reaching for Lark's pack. Suppose she'd taken something into the bathroom with her—she'd been so cheerful—so eager for a good meal—last meal and all . . .

"Okay," Lark called. "It's all yours."

Gillian pushed the pack guiltily away as Lark came out of the bathroom, her slight body wrapped in a towel. "The pressure's pretty good and the water's hot. Be careful to mix it first. You only have to turn the faucet a little and the temperature changes." Lark's face was flushed from the heat of the shower and her eyes were shining. Again, she looked more like ten or twelve than fourteen. "What's the matter? My face still dirty?"

"No," said Gillian. "Not at all."

"Funny-looking, then, I bet." Lark sat down on the bed tailor-fashion, opposite Gillian, draping a corner of the towel modestly between her legs. "Must be funny-looking."

"No. Not funny-looking, either." Gillian wanted to hug her, but she got up instead. "Cute."

Like a child, she thought in the shower, letting the water cascade over her body. Like my child, almost.

Twenty-two

THEY FELL ASLEEP watching television, sprawled on the big bed. Gillian woke up at about three, to find Lark snuggled against her, her head on her shoulder. A test pattern flickered on the screen.

Gillian lay there for several minutes, looking down at Lark, listening to her breathe. Her face was calm now, her mouth relaxed; her hair, tousled from the shower, wisped around her small face. One strand fell near her eyes when she shifted slightly in her sleep. Very gently, Gillian tucked it back, and moved Lark onto the pillows. She got up, used the bathroom, and turned off the TV and the light. Then she climbed back into bed, wishing she could call Suze.

But so far, so good, she thought. So far, nothing horrible has happened.

The rising sun woke them both, its light streaming around the ill-fitting shade. Gillian opened her eyes to see Lark's smiling into her own, and she smiled back. "Good morning, little one," she said. "Sleep okay?"

Lark nodded. Then her eyes filled with tears and she turned away from Gillian, her knees drawn up to her chest, sobbing.

"What is it?" Gillian asked, dismayed, touching Lark's shoulder. "Lark, what is it? Tell me!"

Lark shook her head violently.

Helplessly, Gillian rubbed her back, then put her arms around her and let her cry. Finally, when Lark's sobs eased, Gillian went around to the other side of the bed and, moving Lark over, sat next to her so she could see her. Lark's face was red and swollen with crying; she was still hiccupping softly. "Lark," she said again. "Lark, please. What is it?"

"It was so warm with you next to me in a real bed. So warm, so safe. Like, like you really loved me."

"I do really love you. All I ever had was a big sister. I told you, now I have a little sister, too."

"But you're going to send me away." Lark sat up and flung her arms around Gillian. "I'll never see you again. Gillie, please. Please don't send me away. Please take me to Oregon. I'll—I'll cook for you or—or something. I could get a job; you wouldn't have to pay for me. Please take me." She paused, then added, "I'll do it again if you don't. You're all I have, you . . ."

"Lark," said Gillian, forcing her rising fear down and hating herself for being harsh, but knowing she had to be. "I'm not all you have. You have Jackie, you have Lady, you have your aunt . . ."

"It's you I want."

"You have me, too. I told you that. I told you that

221

I'll always care about you and keep in touch with you. But you can't come to Oregon, you just can't." She put her hands gently on both sides of Lark's face. "You should go back to Jackie. He needs you; he needs you to help him grow up. And you need him, too."

"No. I need you."

Gillian hesitated; she'd imagined many scenes with Lark, but not this one. "I'm not going to abandon you, Lark," she said carefully. "But you should have more help than I can give you. I'd be afraid I'd do something wrong if I tried to go on helping you. I don't want to do anything to harm you, anything bad for you. And I'm just not sure if—oh, blast, this sounds so patronizing and cold; I don't mean to sound that way, like I'm superior or something!"

Gillian got up and moved away, avoiding Lark's wet and lonely eyes; she leaned against the tiny bureau, trying to put her tumbled thoughts in order. "Look," she said finally, struggling to combine honesty and tact, "I think what it is, at least partly, is that I'm scared. I'm terrified of what sometimes goes on inside you." She tried to smile. "Hey, Onion, you have to admit you're complicated and moody. I'm moody sometimes, too; I know how it feels. But your moods are—bigger, somehow, and you shift so fast sometimes, from one feeling to another, as if those wonderful onion layers sort of—not come unfastened, really, but sort of melt together, push up into each other . . ."

Lark was staring at her. "How do you know?"

"I don't know. I was guessing. Am I right?"

Lark nodded. "Oh, yes! That's how it feels sometimes. Just when everything is really okay, when I'm happy. Then something else—it's like it tries to take over, to force its way into the happiness. As if something inside me says I don't deserve it, it isn't right. I don't think I'm really crazy, but I . . ." She shook her head. "More and more with you," she said in a low voice, "I did feel happy. I wanted to live. But then I'd say no, it won't last, she'll go away, she doesn't really care, and I knew I'd be better off dead, as soon as Jackie was safe. But I liked being with you and—and you did seem to care, and then I wasn't sure; I didn't know if I wanted to be dead or not. Some of what you said began making sense, and I began feeling maybe I was okay after all, and maybe there were some good things around after all. And good people, like you. So I'd say, just wait a little more, wait and see . . ."

"Good," said Gillian softly. "Oh, Lark, that's wonderful! That's what lots of people say, I think, when things are bad. 'Wait and see—things might get better later.' Why not wait? Otherwise, you might miss something special."

Lark took Gillian's hands. "I—I think I do want to be alive. And strong, like you. I think I do. I used to think that when I'd gotten Jackie settled there'd be nothing left to do or be. But I wanted to be with you. I wanted to eat that steak. I even wanted to have a shower! So—so maybe you're right that people can change things. You've changed me." She let go Gillian's hands and picked at the bedcovers. "I know you're right about me, about my moods. I know I'm—what's the word? Unstable? But maybe I'm not quite so much so anymore. I do think maybe I could be okay now. I guess I didn't really mean it about—you know, about trying it again if I couldn't go with you. But your going away scares me. I'm scared anyway, Gillian. It's scary, living. And without you . . ."

"You won't be without me. I'll call; we'll write letters. I could see you, even, sometimes, on vacations." She put her hand on Lark's shoulder. "Lark, life *is* scary. For everyone, lots of times. I think you could be okay, too. But I also think you need help. To make things easier, Lark. You've had it tough for too long a time."

Lark got up and moved as far away from Gillian as was possible in the tiny room. "A shrink," she said finally, just as Gillian was fearing she wasn't going to speak at all.

"Maybe. Or maybe just a psychologist."

"I hate shrinks." Lark turned, smiling wanly, like a child again, like Jackie. "They make you say things; they have all kinds of crazy ideas. That one at the hospital . . . They think all girls are in love with their fathers." She laughed, adult again, a short, bitter laugh. "A lot they know."

"Not all shrinks are like that. Margie went to one long ago who was, and she hated him so much our parents sent her to another. And the second one was fine. Margie said the second one knew what she was thinking better than she did herself, but that it was okay."

"How long did she go for?"

"Not too long. The thing I remember most is that she said Dr. Whoever-it-was never made her feel guilty, and said that the things she was worried about weren't wrong or bad. Margie used to have all kinds of imaginings, fantasies, I guess you'd call them. And some of them scared her. But the shrink helped her

224

understand them, and she's fine now. She still has a good imagination, but it doesn't frighten her anymore."

"I'd like to be fine," Lark said softly.

"I'm sure you can be. You're quite a person, you really are." Gillian smiled. "You're even gifted, remember?"

"You won't leave me? I mean, you'll write to me, visit me, if I go back to my aunt's?"

"Try to keep me away."

"I'm scared."

"I know. But you know what else? You're also very brave. You were brave to take care of Jackie the way you did, even though you were hurting inside. I'm scared, too, sometimes, Lark; everyone is. As I said, life is often scary. The important thing is being able to handle it. And you will. I know you will." She went up to Lark and hugged her, then looked down at her. "Okay? My brave Lark?"

For a moment Lark clung to Gillian—but Gillian felt no sobs this time.

Then Lark lifted her head and smiled. "Okay," she whispered. "I'll try."

Twenty-three

THEY HAD EGGS and toast in the cabin, then did
the dishes and checked out, waking the indifferent
owner in order to pay him and return the key. And
then they drove through the early morning, back to
Laconia. The sun was only partway up in the sky
when they started, and the air was still cool and
misty.

Gillian felt drained and had to fight to stay awake.
Dear God, she prayed silently several times, let me be
right; let her be okay.

Jackie and Lady were playing outside the house
when Gillian drove up with Lark, and they tumbled
all over each other getting to the car. "Larkie, Larkie,
Larkie!" Jackie shouted, running to her with his arms
open, while Lady pranced and barked. When Lark's
aunt, a tall, capable-looking woman in a faded but

clean flowered housedress, came outside, boy, girl, and dog were locked in a fast embrace.

Gillian met the aunt's smiling eyes. "Thank you," said the aunt, "for bringing her back. I've called their mother. She said Lark could stay here, too, if she came back."

"I think Lark needs help," Gillian said, reluctant to broach the subject without preamble, but not sure she'd have a chance to say it less bluntly. "A counselor. Psychiatrist, maybe. She's a wonderful girl, but . . ."

"She'll have help," Lark's aunt said, her eyes darkening. "She'll have all the help she needs. I'm not going to see either of them destroyed, or have them just turn out weak, like their mother. Never you worry—Miss Harrison."

The irony in her voice told Gillian she hadn't believed Lark's story about her being a teacher, or didn't believe it now that she'd seen her. But the woman held out her hand to Gillian, even so, and grasped Gillian's firmly. "Thank you," she said. "I don't want to pry, and I won't pry. But it seems to me a lot went on here that I should be grateful to you for. I want you to know that I am."

"That's okay," Gillian said clumsily, embarrassed. "Really, I—I'll keep in touch. May I?"

Lark's aunt nodded.

Gillian turned to Lark, who was now standing nearby, one arm around Jackie. "Hear that? I'll keep in touch. I promise. You promise, too."

Lark ran to Gillian and hugged her hard, then brought Jackie into the hug, and Lady, and by the time Gillian drove off again, her eyes were so full of tears she had to pull over a couple of blocks away and cry.

And then she dried her eyes, lifted her head, and started the long drive back to Pookatasset, to face whatever it was she was going to have to face there.

It had indeed been worth it.